ASSIGNMENT: MARRIAGE

ASSIGNMENT: MARRIAGE

BY

JODI DAWSON

MILLS & BOON®

First published in Great Britain 2003
Large Print edition 2004
Harlequin Mills & Boon Limited,
Eton House, 18-24 Paradise Road,
Richmond, Surrey TW9 1SR

© Jodi Dawson 2003

ISBN 0 263 18082 4

Set in Times Roman 17½ on 19 pt.
16-0604-40351

Printed and bound in Great Britain
by Antony Rowe Ltd, Chippenham, Wiltshire

CHAPTER ONE

DANIEL WEST had often been told he was hardheaded. Unfortunately, the iron skillet that knocked him on the head happened to be harder. He yelped in stunned surprise before slumping against the cool bricks of the house.

A miniscule figure wrapped in layers of stars peered at him through the hazy moonlight. Daniel shook his head in an effort to clear his vision and focus on the face of his assailant.

Bad idea.

The throbbing on the fringes of his awareness became an incessant beat. He slid along the surface of the wall until his backside settled into the crunch of fallen leaves littering the damp earth. Moisture seeped through his jeans. The aroma of bacon surrounded and confused him.

Tipping his head back, Daniel watched as the floating fairy of the iron skillet lowered her weapon of choice and reached toward him. Gentle fingers probed the area on his forehead where he realized the granddaddy of all lumps now protruded.

Eyes squeezed tight to still the vertigo threatening to topple him into the chrysanthemums, Daniel sensed the surreal minx kneel next to him.

''I'll let you decide.'' Her steady voice sounded loud in the quiet of the night.

''Decide what?''

Daniel opened his eyes and stared into the brazen, green eyes of the lady of the house. He knew he faced his target. Katherine Bennett—the mouse who might lead him to the cheese. Her distant tie to the suspected mastermind of a recent rash of bank robberies was all he had to go on.

Now his cover was blown. *Great job, Sherlock.* Daniel forced himself to focus on her statement as he peered up at her.

Katherine stood and gripped the skillet handle with both hands. "Do I call the police and report you for the rotten Peeping Tom you are or call an ambulance to treat your concussion?"

"I'm not a Peeping Tom." Daniel tried to straighten.

"And your explanation for lurking around my house in the dark would be…?"

Now, how to answer her question? The truth would likely earn him another blow to the head. Daniel pushed into a kneeling position and grimaced as heavy dew penetrated the knees of his pants. He reached a hand in Katherine Bennett's direction to reassure himself she was real.

A growl rumbled from somewhere behind her and stopped him cold.

"Buster is my watchdog." Katherine glanced backward and gave a soft, two-toned whistle. A beast of a dog loped to her side. Its impossibly long tongue lolled comically to one side.

Daniel rocked back on his heels. Things kept getting better and better. Time to face the music. He reached toward his back pocket to show her some identification.

In a flash, the dog hit him like a line backer for the Denver Broncos and he lay sprawled on his back, staring into the drooling mouth of eighty pounds of angry canine. Daniel decided to refrain from any movement. Even breathing was risky.

"Heard you…have rooms…available." He spoke out of the corner of his mouth.

"You want a room?" Katherine looked doubtful. "Why didn't you come to the front door?"

Daniel glanced at the dog. Katherine stood and performed a subtle hand motion that caused the creature to move from Daniel's chest.

''The lady at the chamber of commerce who recommended you mentioned most people use your back entrance.'' Daniel eased into a sitting position and used a hand to brace his forehead. It wasn't an outright lie. He *had* talked to the helpful woman.

Katherine crossed her arms and raised a skeptical eyebrow. ''Mary recommended my bed-and-breakfast to you?'' Her doubt was clear.

Daniel forced himself to think and keep his stories straight. The pounding in his head didn't make it easier. ''I asked for something relaxing and private. Mary said the Naked Moon Tearoom was the place and that you were the queen of relaxation.''

Katherine hesitated a moment, then offered her hand. A small smile tipped her lips upward. "If Mary sent you over, how can I turn you away?"

He stared at the hand she believed would help him stand.

Katherine's expression showed exasperation. "I'm stronger than I look."

Daniel's hand swallowed hers. She tugged and he stood. Sort of. His open palm slapped the wall as he attempted to slow the spinning.

Katherine stepped under his free arm and the top of her head barely reached his chin. "I'm sorry. You came looking for relaxation and I bashed you on the head. Let me help you inside." She glanced up at him with a frown. "You're not a lawyer, are you?"

"No." Daniel leaned into her soft warmth. Deceptive softness. He knew the strength behind her swing. "Why?"

"Don't want you planning a lawsuit against me."

Her honesty surprised him. In his line of work Daniel didn't encounter it often. Too bad he couldn't show her the same courtesy. Until he discerned the nature of her connection to Filcher, honesty wasn't an option.

Painstakingly, they stumbled toward the back of the two-story Victorian house. Rounding the corner, Daniel blinked in the glow of light next to the door. Peering down, he took advantage of the first-clear view of his hostess. His quarry.

Daniel stared. The black-and-white photo he had of Miss Katherine Bennett didn't do her justice. Her unbound black hair brushed the swell of her breasts and draped halfway down her back. The filmy robe she wore clung to her curves, the fabric was almost sheer, the color of a night sky sprinkled with silver stars. Her freshly scrubbed face glowed with good health and the exertion of helping him. She was a looker.

Katherine glanced upward and caught him staring. Rather than looking embarrassed, she tilted her head and stared back at him. Her eyes seemed to offer a challenge. How much was real and how much was his imagination, Daniel didn't know.

He cleared his throat and looked away. ''Uh, I don't suppose you'd consider renting me a room?''

Katherine laughed. The sound surrounded him in the stillness of twilight, making him feel welcome. ''If you're willing to risk it, how can I refuse?''

Step one accomplished—infiltrate the residence. ''Uh, why were you in the yard with a skillet?''

''I was feeding the chrysanthemums.'' She reached for the doorknob.

Daniel stopped short. The dossier on this woman hadn't mentioned mental instability. ''Excuse me?''

''My aunt always slipped a bit of bacon grease to them to keep them happy. But she said it only works after dark,'' Katherine said in a matter-of-fact tone as she pulled the door open.

Welcoming warmth poured from the house, sprinkled with tantalizing aromas as they stepped into a large kitchen. Glass jars lined every inch of available space, filled with…things. The contents resembled dead grass and bug parts. The case grew stranger by the second.

Katherine led him to a chair and helped him onto it. She retrieved a bag of frozen corn from the freezer. ''Hold this on your bump and I'll brew something to help your head.''

Daniel's gaze followed her shapely figure to the monstrosity of a stove, a throwback to another century. ''Brew? Never mind. I'll just toss a couple of aspirin back.''

Katherine turned and stared at him, green eyes filled with censure. ''Mary must not have told you the other half, the main focus, of my business.''

''Only that you run a bed-and-breakfast.'' Daniel silently cursed, for the thousandth time, the lack of detailed information in her file. There hadn't been time to gather more background before he'd headed into the field.

''I operate a tearoom, specializing in natural teas and herbal infusions for healing.'' Katherine watched his face for a reaction.

He was careful to keep his expression neutral. ''That's unusual.''

She turned back to the stove and ignited a flame beneath a large enamel teapot.

Tea. That explained the stuff in the glass jars. It wasn't as simple to understand the woman's trust. Daniel hadn't offered his name, only a referral, and she'd taken him in.

Of course, the hulk of a dog was all the protection an attractive woman needed. And Buster still glared at him.

"The name's West, Daniel West." He started to stand, but thought better of it when the room wavered.

Katherine shook his outstretched hand. "Katherine Bennett, folks call me Kat. It's all I answer to, so you may as well use it."

Daniel watched her move about the room. Wonder what's under that robe? He tore his gaze away and stared at the ancient icebox to take his mind off further personal reflections on Katherine…Kat.

"How long are you staying in Sugar Gulch?" Kat stirred the amber liquid in her cup.

"Um…I'm not certain. I'm a freelance writer, doing an article on the local area." Daniel spun the story he'd invented to explain his presence in the small Colorado mountain town. "I'll interview local residents and visit sites of interest. Maybe I could interview you?"

Why did he feel like a creep for lying? Sure, his job working undercover for a national insurance firm required he mislead people, but he didn't have to like it.

"I'm afraid the only thing I'm an expert on is tea. But you'll want to talk to Elizabeth, my next-door neighbor. She knows anything and everything that's happened in these parts for at least the past hundred years."

Kat offered the steaming cup. "Sugar?"

"You bet."

"One lump or two?"

Daniel grimaced and touched the tender spot on his head. "I already have one, maybe just one more." He looked at the liquid skeptically.

Kat plopped the sugar cube into his tea. "I'm not trying to poison you. And there are no dead bodies buried in the cellar." Kat shook her head at his blank stare. "Never mind. This is an herbal infusion, a tea of sorts. Peppermint and mandarin to help with your headache and discomfort.''

Daniel held the cup and stared into the swirling contents. How did he end up in these crazy messes?

Kat watched the perplexing man stare at the tea with apprehension in his gorgeous blue eyes. No, blue didn't even begin to describe them. Piercing, they seemed to look through her nightclothes to stare at her bare skin beneath.

Could this be the man the tea leaves predicted this morning? At the time, Kat had laughed. A man was the last thing she needed right now. Avoiding the pesky advances of Chad Filcher kept her busy enough. In fact, the town banker had become downright annoying. She grinned. Maybe she ought to try the skillet trick on him.

Daniel blew across the surface of the hot liquid. Kat imagined the ripples that would spread in front of his well-shaped lips. Echoing ripples of sensation shivered up Kat's spine.

I don't need this.

Kat spun back to the stove and poured another cup of tea, chamomile and lavender to help her relax and induce sleep. *Yeah, right.* As though she'd be able to sleep knowing the drop-dead, handsome hunk slept under the same roof. She sipped the tea anyway.

The hair at the nape of her neck raised. He was staring at her—she sensed it clear to her toes.

Daniel broke the intimate silence. "Can I see my room? Think I'd better lie down."

Kat turned around and surveyed his empty cup with satisfaction. He'd soon feel better and would sleep soundly. "There are two bedrooms on this level besides my own. This is a slow weekend, so you're my only guest."

"Stairs don't sound like a great idea anyway. Good thing you only clipped me or I'd be out cold."

Heat crept up Kat's neck. Bashing him on the head hadn't been premeditated. Instinct had propelled Kat's arm when she'd glimpsed him in the dark. Then again, it was better than having Buster clamp a mouthful of teeth on the man's leg. She was lucky he wasn't threatening to sue her.

He stood, wobbling a bit. Kat set down her tea and stepped forward. "I'll help you."

"Thanks."

She wrapped an arm around his waist. Tall, he had to be at least six feet. And in shape. No extra flab around his middle.

Kat blushed as she realized she was evaluating him as though he was livestock on the auction block rather than a flesh-and-blood man.

* * *

Buster padded behind them as they passed into the dimly lit hall.

Thankfully the suite nearest her room was vacant, in case Daniel required help during the night, Kat pushed the door open with her foot. ''Do you need your luggage tonight?''

''I'll get by until morning.'' Daniel switched the bedside lamp on and eased away from her arm. ''Hmm…you smell good.''

''It's the lamp.''

''What?''

''There's an oil ring on the bulb. It holds Immortelle oil. Good for increasing your dreams.'' For heaven's sake, she sounded like a babbling idiot. Why did this man unbalance her? She needed to get away from his unnerving presence.

Kat stepped back to leave. Unfortunately, Buster sat directly behind her. His yelp of pain sent Kat stumbling into Daniel. His eyes widened with surprise when she slammed into his chest and pushed him backward onto the mattress.

Kat groaned. The ultimate humiliation. Instead of projecting the image of a cool businesswoman, she appeared more like a sex-starved nympho. Sprawled on top of Daniel West, Kat stared down at him like an idiot. One side of his mouth quirked up, followed by the other. The chest beneath her shook gently, then more noticeably. Uh-oh. She'd given the poor man a heart attack.

Daniel's mouth opened and he laughed. A deep, masculine sound. He continued to laugh until she finally allowed a small smile to curve her lips.

Daniel's eyes twinkled up at her. ''Lady, are you always a walking disaster or is tonight a special occasion?''

''Must be you.'' Embarrassed, Kat pushed up on her arms and wriggled backward until her feet touched the floor.

"Buster and I will leave before you end up in the hospital."

She walked to the door, then glanced back to see Daniel watching her from the bed. Kat gave him a weak smile and closed the door. She leaned her back against it, taking deep breaths as her body pulsed with currents of sensuality.

Daniel was dangerous to her peace of mind. And body.

It was going to be a long night.

Daniel shook his head. Kat's seemingly innocent accidents were distracting. She was a pro. The little wiggle when she'd slid off him had nearly sent him through the roof. Everywhere their bodies had touched ignited with fire.

He shook his head. He needed to remember the reason for his presence in this town and whom Kat might be involved with. Katherine Bennett could be the key to busting the string of bank robberies wide open. And he could use a break on the case.

The bank's corporate office had requested Daniel because of his reputation for cracking internal fraud cases, and no curvaceous package of pure herbal dynamite was going to distract him.

Turning his thoughts to the coming day, Daniel undressed, dropped his clothes on the floor, and placed his wallet under the pillow. Slipping between flannel sheets, he forced his mind to focus on the mission that lay ahead and turned out the light.

Several moments passed before his eyes adjusted to the gloom. I should lock the door.

Too tired to move, he dismissed the thought and stared at the ceiling. He had exactly one week to come up with major progress on the case for the company before the Feds took over. That wouldn't look good on his record. Not good at all. The last thing he needed in his life, or on this investigation, was a ditzy woman screwing things up.

Daniel had learned the hard way just how much a woman could mess with your mind and your career. His engagement to Vivian had ended over six months ago. Nothing he'd done had ever measured up to her family's high society standards. Not his job, and certainly not his lifestyle.

Daniel grimaced in the dark, remembering Vivian's pouting fits if he'd tried to take time for mountain biking or camping. Instead, she'd pushed him to take a position with Global Insurance, hoping advancement and higher pay would come rapidly. What made it worse was that he'd actually gone along with most of the changes she'd demanded in his life.

When she'd tearfully admitted to being in love with her lawyer, Daniel had whooped with joy. Not quite the reaction she'd expected. But her confession had crystallized their relationship for him.

They'd been comfortable together, nothing more.

Daniel wished her well, and meant it. Then he'd vowed to never make such a mistake again. Love meant changing who you were, and no way would he be spineless for a woman again.

Tempting she might be, but Katherine Bennett was only a possible means of solving this case. That's all he'd let her be. That is, so long as she didn't wale at him with her frying pan again. Daniel touched the swelling on his forehead. The throbbing had subsided, just like Kat promised. If the scented oil worked as well as the tea, he was in for a long night of dreaming. He frowned. Vivid dreams of Kat were a distraction he didn't want.

Kat latched the back door and gave Buster a treat. He deserved it—the overgrown mutt offered security—and friendship. He'd defended her tonight. Daniel West didn't need to know the dog was more likely to lick him to death than attack. Daniel hadn't known, and that was what mattered.

Scratching the furry head pushed under her hand, Kat allowed her thoughts to wander. She'd managed to keep her mind off her nocturnal visitor while cleaning the kitchen and mixing dough for the next morning's cinnamon rolls. But she wouldn't be able to much longer— Elizabeth wouldn't let her.

The older woman would dance a gleeful jig when she glimpsed Daniel and noted the absence of a wedding band on his finger. Elizabeth nagged incessantly about Kat's love life or lack at it. Exasperated, she wondered why people assumed a woman wasn't complete without a man. Kat enjoyed her business and her life.

Intimate involvement with a guest was the last thing she should be thinking of. So why did tantalizing images of being sprawled atop Daniel West tease her? She glanced down at the cause of the little accident. Buster was probably in cahoots with Elizabeth.

Maybe Kat would slip Buster another treat. Sensual zings were nonexistent in Kat's life, and tonight's had been a whopper. The brief contact with Daniel's hard body had burned through her nightgown and robe as though they were no more substantial than early morning fog...just a reminder she was close to becoming the old maid her dear great-aunt had been and Elizabeth remained.

Maybe she *would* lure Daniel into a torrid affair for the brief time he'd be here...and pigs might fly!

Kat had no idea how to lure a man into a casual involvement. Since she'd never had an affair, much less a torrid one, she wouldn't know where to begin. And she wanted, deserved more. So, like the proverbial princess in an ivory tower, she'd wait for true love.

Or a close facsimile.

Kat shook her head and gave up. She'd never get to sleep. Might as well catch up on the laundry. And since Daniel's jeans were damp and smeared with bacon grease from his unplanned frolic in the flower-bed, washing them might help make up for the bodily injury she'd inflicted.

She paused outside the door to his room. Buster tipped his head and looked at her with confusion. Kat patted his head and whispered reassurances. "I know I don't usually go into the guest's rooms, but I did cause him to get dirty. And I should make sure he's recovering from his injuries."

Kat twisted the glass knob and eased the door open, praying her guest was a sound sleeper. She peered into the dark room and breathed a sigh of relief.

Daniel's eyes were closed, one arm flung above his head. His steady breathing reassured her. She tiptoed to the pile of clothing next to the bed and reached for his jeans.

The reason for her illicit visit gripped in her fingers, Kat straightened. Though she had planned a quick exit, she stood instead and stared at the chiseled features of the man on the bed.

Moonlight filtered through the lace curtains and turned his tousled blond hair to pale silver. He needed a haircut. And, yet, on Daniel, the extra length only added to his raw masculinity.

Daniel moved restlessly in his sleep. The sheet slipped down to his waist, revealing the expanse of his muscled chest. Golden hairs sprinkled his tanned skin. Kat's breath caught in her throat. She was trapped between the urgent need to flee and the hope his sheet might slip a little farther.

Kat gave herself a mental shake. She was twenty-eight years old for crying out loud. Her heart thundering in her ears, she backed towards the door. She needed to leave. There wasn't enough air in the room.

Kat risked one last peek, then stepped into the hall and gently shut the door behind her.

Buster nudged her with his wet nose, seeming to sense her disquiet.

"It's okay, boy." Kat steadied the quaver in her voice. "Let's get the laundry going."

If only she were a modern woman. She'd slip back into the room, waken Daniel and…and what?

Forget it. It'd never happen in a million years.

Daniel stared at the closed door. He'd begun to think Kat would never leave. The strain of faking sleep while she stood over him had tightened all of the muscles her tea had relaxed.

What had she been after? He leaned over to peer at his clothing on the floor. His pants were missing. Why in the world would she take his pants?

Unless she hadn't bought his story and was looking for more information. It was a damned good thing he'd had the sense to hide his wallet. She'd be disappointed when she discovered it wasn't there. Served her right.

Daniel eased out of bed and walked to the door. Pressing one ear against the smooth wood, he listened. Rushing water was the only sound. Was she in the shower at this time of night?

Daniel turned the lock and sank onto the edge of the mattress. The only thing he knew at this point was that Kat had to be watched. Behind those innocent, green eyes lurked a sharp mind. He wouldn't let his guard down for a minute.

Too much was at stake.

*　　*　　*

Kat tossed dark colored clothes into the washer while it filled with water. She retrieved Daniel's muddy jeans from the floor and performed the usual pocket search. Washing his wallet wouldn't endear her to him.

A folded paper fell from the front pocket. Kat picked it up, tossed the pants into the washer and closed the lid. She stared at the paper in her hand.

The note was folded once, and she could nearly discern the writing through the paper.

Her fingers opened the paper even as her mind told her it was wrong. Kat's eyes scanned a printed list.

Bank names, from towns around Sugar Gulch. The names tugged at her memory as Kat frowned in concentration. Something nibbled at the edge of her subconscious.

Then it hit her. No wonder the names bothered her. They'd been in the news the past few weeks—because they'd all been robbed in a string of unsolved holdups.

So why were they on a list in the pocket of a man who had been lurking outside her house? In the middle of the night?

The answer was simple. The first man to ignite her jets in years was a felon.

She'd been lusting after an outlaw. Perfect. Just perfect.

CHAPTER TWO

KAT rubbed morning grit from her eyes. A glance at the bedside clock confirmed the early hour. Unfortunately, she had no more answers now than when sleep had claimed her two hours earlier.

Locking her bedroom door seemed foolish in the light of morning. Surely there was a perfectly logical explanation for the paper in Daniel's pocket. She'd pay close attention today and discover what it was.

Buster stirred on the floor near the foot of her bed and stretched with a protesting yawn before snuggling back into his blanket for a few final minutes of sleep. If only life were as simple as a good meal and the occasional snooze.

Kat folded both arms behind her head and stared at the crocheted canopy above her. The elevated bed was a private haven. A place where she did her best thinking and dreaming.

The soothing scent of lavender surrounded her as it drifted from the sachet tucked inside her pillowcase. The familiar aroma calmed her, helped her active imagination to slow its headlong rush.

Reluctantly, Kat sat upright. It was time to prepare for Elizabeth. Their morning tea ritual hadn't altered in the years Kat had known the woman. Luckily for Kat, they shared a belief in tea as the elixir of the soul, as well as a deep affection for one another.

They were family. In the way that truly mattered in the heart. Kat silently thanked her guardian angel for directing her path back toward home after college. Her degree in business administration left her more than qualified to run her aunt's business. And Kat had the memories of time spent with Aunt Bernice before her death.

All of the seeming unrelated events had enabled her to stay close to Elizabeth. Whenever Kat thought she might be missing anything by coming home rather than seeking a high dollar, high-energy career in a big city she simply looked around Sugar Gulch. Here, people she cared about surrounded her.

Whenever Elizabeth bemoaned Kat's lack of interest in a romantic relationship with any of the single men in town, she simply changed the subject. After the last foray into a serious relationship during her final year of college, Kat was content to not worry about things that took her mind off her main objectives. Watching over Elizabeth, running the bed-and-breakfast, and her natural healing teas were things she could count on.

Swinging bare legs over the edge of the bed, Kat used the two-step stool to lower herself onto the chilly, hardwood floor. Shivering, she patted Buster before stepping into the bathroom. A hot shower would clear away the cobwebs that remained in her mind, then she'd be better prepared to face her suspicious guest.

Thirty minutes later, Kat opened the front door for Buster and retrieved the morning paper from the porch.

"Morning."

Daniel's soft greeting startled her. Kat clutched the newspaper protectively against her chest and turned to see him seated on the porch swing. Some super spy she'd make. "You...you're up early." The squeak in her voice grated in the hushed morning air. She was thankful for the warm sweater draped over her shoulders, it kept the chill from stealing the pleasure from the early hour.

"Best part of the day."

"My favorite, too." *Good, establish common ground. Keep him talking.* "I popped cinnamon rolls into the oven, they'll be out in ten minutes.''

Daniel stared at her with obvious questions in his eyes. Had she alerted him to her suspicions? Kat reviewed her actions and words. No, she'd been careful.

Buster bounded onto the porch, coming to an abrupt halt when he spotted Daniel. Dog and man eyed each other. The hair along Buster's back stood upright. Legs braced, he gave a sharp bark.

''Knock it off, Buster.'' Kat laced her fingers through his collar and tugged. He turned and settled at her feet, but kept his attention glued on Daniel.

Daniel's lips curved into a smile. Kat stared at the fullness of his lower lip, the sharp line of his jaw. He was too good-looking for her peace of mind. Like a piece of decadent chocolate—desirable, but bound to cause regrets later.

''Buster's a regular knight-in-shining armor.'' The smile took the sting from his words.

"He was my great-aunt's dog. I'm afraid Aunt Bernice trained him to be wary of men." Kat wished Daniel's intense focus would turn elsewhere. Her skin tingled beneath his gaze. "You mentioned researching an article—do you work for a paper?"

"No, I'm self-employed."

"Where are you from?"

"Denver." Daniel pushed against the wooden planks with his foot and the swing resumed its motion.

Kat stared into the mist-shrouded yard. Subterfuge didn't come easily. She glanced at Daniel through her lashes. His arms stretched along the back of the swing, his shirt pulled across his chest and emphasized the width of his shoulders. *He has to spend time pumping iron.*

"Do you like it?"

Kat's head snapped up and she stared at him with her mouth hanging open and a burning heat stinging her cheeks. He'd noticed her stare and read her lustful thoughts.

''Small town life—do you like it?'' Daniel repeated the question she'd obviously missed.

Kat relaxed her stiff shoulders. After all, the man wasn't a mind reader. ''I love it. Wouldn't live anywhere else.''

''Why not?''

Rather than answer his question, Kat asked one of her own. ''Do you like your job?''

''Yes.'' Daniel stopped swinging.

''Why?''

''It's rewarding.''

Kat leaned against a porch pillar and crossed her ankles. ''That's the way I feel about Sugar Gulch and small town life. Not only do I have great friends and neighbors, but I enjoy the feeling I get when someone comes to me for advice and I send them home with a tea that can help.''

Daniel rubbed his palm along his whiskered jaw, curiosity and skepticism in his eyes. "So you're the local witch doctor?"

"I prefer natural healer," Kat answered tersely. Tension pushed her backbone straighter.

Daniel didn't seem to notice. "How did you learn this natural tea stuff?"

"My great-aunt taught me as she raised me."

"She lives with you?"

"No, she passed on a year ago and left me the tearoom."

He looked into her eyes. "I'm sorry. You must miss her."

"Oh I do, but we talk regularly."

Daniel arched his brows upward.

Kat smiled. She enjoyed the play of emotions across his strong features, the confusion in his eyes. "I'm not a crazy— I just talk out loud sometimes. It feels as though Aunt Bernice is still listening. She never wanted me to grieve.''

Doubt still remained on Daniel's face. He probably thought she was certifiable, or at least a bit off.

Kat patted her thigh to attract Buster's attention. ''Come on boy, time for you to eat.''

Daniel stepped onto the sidewalk in front of the house then turned back. ''Kat?''

She turned to face him.

''Thanks for washing my jeans. I'll be back in after I get my luggage.'' He walked toward a car parked at the curb.

Kat sighed and entered the house. Why couldn't she shake this attraction to the man when he obviously had no romantic interest in her? A true soul mate would have recognized her instantly...wouldn't he? It didn't make a difference—there was no room for a man in her life anyway.

She set the small table in the kitchen and listened to Daniel's footsteps echoing in the hallway before the door to his room closed. Kat hoped he'd finish the story on Sugar Gulch soon. Distraction she didn't need.

''Well, Buster, what do you think? He thinks I'm a witch doctor and I beat him on the head with a skillet. Should I ask him out?''

Buster lifted his nose from the bowl and tipped his head.

''My thoughts exactly, he's too uptight. Straight-laced. No imagination.'' Kat set a teapot in the center of the table. She meant what she'd said to Buster…so why did she have the urge to sneak into Daniel's room and push him backward onto the bed again?

Daniel yanked the stubborn zipper open on his suitcase, automatically lifting clothing and tossing it into drawers. His focus returned to his hostess, and possible suspect. She was a study in contradictions. Soft as forbidden sin and tough as iron, modern woman and imaginative sprite.

The blow to his head must have been harder than he'd thought.

Daniel slammed the drawer closed. He'd have to watch his step and cover his back. Keeping his sexual appetite under control around Kat was going to be tough. It seemed to have taken on a life of its own. And distraction was something he didn't have time for. Questioning Kat hadn't produced any new information pertinent to the investigation.

He had a thief to catch. Even if that thief turned out to be Kat Bennett.

Kat continued icing warm cinnamon rolls when the back door opened on stiff hinges. "Morning, Elizabeth."

"Who is he?" As always, Elizabeth skipped social niceties and jumped straight to the middle of the lake. She didn't waste time dipping a toe to test the waters.

Kat didn't have to guess who her friend was talking about. A number of Elizabeth's windows looked into Kat's yard, so she must have seen Daniel on the porch or entering the house.

"Daniel West. A guest—he arrived late last night." Kat hoped that would answer all of her questions.

She knew better.

"Now, Katherine, I wasn't born yesterday. I can see the purple in your aura. It happened." Elizabeth's nose twitched with delight and a soft flush covered the paper-thin skin of her cheeks. "You're interested in him. Don't bother to deny it."

"Just my overactive imagination. Doesn't mean a thing." *No way can it mean anything.*

Elizabeth chortled with delight. "About time, I'd say. I was afraid you'd end a dried-up old maid like me."

Kat plopped into a chair and rested her elbows on the table, hoping to distract Elizabeth by using bad manners. ''You're nothing of the sort. You're a vibrant, beautiful, involved—''

''Now, don't go trying to divert me. You know it won't work.'' Elizabeth laid a hand atop Kat's on the table and gave a light squeeze. ''Who does he remind you of?''

Kat grinned and shook her head. ''Matt Dillon.'' Elizabeth resembled a human bulldog with a juicy bone. Once focused on something, she'd dig until satisfied with the answers.

''Matt Dillon?'' Watery eyes gazed at her in perplexity.

''Like in 'Gunsmoke,' the old television show. The town sheriff.'' She patiently explained.

''Ah, sounds sexy and mysterious.'' Elizabeth twirled the strand of beads hanging about her neck. "What are you going to do?"

Kat shrugged. "Nothing."

"Why not?" Elizabeth's startled tone attracted Buster's attention. She absently rubbed his head.

"Something's not...right." Kat frowned, not wanting to share the list she'd discovered, but unsure why.

"You think Chad Filcher is more your type?"

"No, Chad Filcher is definitely not my type." Kat shuddered, recalling the banker's clammy hands that always seemed to be touching her arm or shoulder.

Mention of the bank president's name pulled Kat's thoughts back to earth with a solid thump of reality. He'd pursued her for the past several months and she'd gently rebuffed every advance. Now, Kat needed to approach him for help. Not the best situation to be in.

Without the bank's extension on her mortgage payments, Kat would lose the tearoom. It was very odd. Aunt Bernice hadn't been organized, but the missing account was out of character, even for her. The money set aside to clear the mortgage had failed to surface after her aunt died. Kat had managed for two years on a shoestring budget, but final payoff to the bank loomed dark on the horizon.

"Never thought of *Chad* romantically, did you?" Elizabeth harped on about the banker.

"Of course not, but—"

"No buts about it. Let me meet this Daniel fellow. I'll judge for myself." Elizabeth raised a delicate, blue-veined hand in a gesture of finality. The conversation was over. For now.

Kat heard a door open. Daniel was coming, and it would be impossible for him to avoid Elizabeth's inquisition. Kat smiled. Maybe she'd learn more about the list in his pocket by listening to her friend question the distracting man than playing sleuth herself.

Daniel didn't miss a step when he spotted the elderly woman seated at the kitchen table with Kat. His new resolve in place, he focused on business and the job he'd been hired to perform. Nothing would divert him, not even if Kat danced naked on the kitchen counter.

Aw, hell, who am I kidding? That would be tough to ignore and a lot of fun to watch. Focus, West, focus.

''Good morning.'' Buster emitted a low growl from under the table. Daniel was tempted to growl back, but he stuck his hand out and approached the newcomer.

Instead of shaking his hand, the white-haired woman pulled it toward her and turned it over. *What the heck?* She studied his palm and ran her fingertips over his lower arm as goose bumps formed on his skin. Daniel raised his eyebrows in Kat's direction.

Kat motioned with her hand and gave an apologetic shrug. "Daniel, I'd like you to meet Elizabeth—my next door neighbor. I mentioned her last night."

Daniel searched his memory. Ah, yes. The woman she'd recommended he interview—an expert on the local area. But why the devil was Elizabeth staring at him? Had he dribbled toothpaste on his chin or shaved his nose off?

"You'll do nicely." Elizabeth smiled up at him and released his hand. Tiny lines radiated from the corners of her eyes.

"I'll do what?" Daniel looked from Kat to Elizabeth.

Elizabeth smiled knowingly. "Why, whatever's necessary, of course."

Daniel nodded. He didn't understand a thing, but humoring the woman couldn't hurt. Kat motioned him to a chair. She stared at him with an intensity that caused a fire to burn low in his belly. He squashed it. No lust. No fantasies. He was here on business. Strictly business.

Kat placed a cup of tea in front of him. Daniel opened his mouth to let her know he preferred coffee to start his day. Strong and stand-a-spoon-in-it thick, but she turned away before he could protest.

''What kind of tea are we drinking this morning?'' Daniel stared at the liquid. The guys on his Saturday Rugby team would get a kick out of Daniel West, front guard, enjoying his morning tea.

''A basic green tea blend with gingko.'' Kat handed a cup to Elizabeth, then took a sip of her own.

''What's gingko?'' Daniel didn't like the sound of it. Probably caused hair to sprout on the sole of a person's foot.

''A tea with ginger to increase alertness. Elizabeth is having the same.'' A grin tugged at the corner of her lips.

He could certainly use more alertness. Daniel sipped the steaming tea. The tang of lemon lingered on his tongue. Not so subtly, he eyed the cinnamon rolls that oozed icing onto the platter.

''Help yourself.'' Kat offered. ''Do you have a plan for where you'll start today?''

''Since it's a weekday most businesses will be open, so I thought I'd start with the library. Research the extent of their archives.'' Daniel watched Kat for her reaction. She revealed nothing as she buttered her roll.

Elizabeth cleared her throat. ''What is it you're looking for?''

''I'm researching the local area.'' He bit into the warm, spiced roll. Heaven. Kat might be crazy, but she could cook for him anytime.

''Daniel's a writer. He's researching the history of Sugar Gulch,'' Kat explained.

''Oh, then you're interested in the past, maybe past lives?'' Elizabeth's smile widened and her eyes seemed to twinkle.

"Not exactly. I'm interested in re-corded, true events. Things based on fac-tual history." Daniel tried to keep the skepticism from his voice. "Kat thought you'd be a knowledgeable source to inter-view."

"Might be. Depends on who's asking, and why." Elizabeth watched him imp-ishly over the rim of her cup.

Kat stood. "I need to get ready for lunchtime tea."

Daniel tried a different tack. "Is there a bank in town?"

He watched Kat's eyes widen as the healthy glow drained from her face. Two bright spots of color perched high on her cheekbones. Interesting.

Kat swallowed. "Why?"

"I need to cash a check, plus they may have records on the town's residents from the nineteenth century."

All three jumped when a knock sounded at the back door.

"Come in," Kat called.

The back door opened and a tall man entered the kitchen. The man's gaze darted about the room before settling on Kat. Daniel watched her stiffen and frown. She obviously wasn't thrilled to see the visitor.

Elizabeth leaned back in her chair, as though to enjoy a show. A mischievous smile settled on her lips.

Kat recovered quickly. "Chad, what brings you by so early?"

"Thought I'd bring you the latest report on the bank's search for your aunt's account." The man stepped into the room and glanced at Daniel, measuring and dismissing him with a look.

"That's thoughtful of you. You know Elizabeth." Kat turned to Daniel. "This is my guest, Daniel West. Daniel, I'd like to introduce Chad Filcher. He's president of the First Bank of Sugar Gulch."

"Morning." Daniel noticed Filcher didn't offer his hand. It fit the information Daniel had on him—aloof and unfriendly. Except when it came to Kat. Was this Kat's boyfriend? Odd, the two didn't seem cozy. No welcoming smile or kiss. In a town that seemed to overflow with neighborliness, Filcher just didn't seem to fit.

"Will you be in town long?" Chad asked in a stilted tone.

"Only long enough to research a story." And catch a crook.

"Good, good." Turning to Kat, the banker moved his lips in a practiced smile. "Would you like to discuss the latest developments here? Or, meet for lunch?"

"I won't be finished here until after lunchtime." Kat glanced at the clock. "How about two o'clock at the bank?"

"I'll expect you." Filcher nodded at Kat and Elizabeth then turned to Daniel and said, "Mr. West, good luck on your research."

The door closed behind him and silence stretched in the kitchen. Kat nibbled at her lower lip, worry creasing her forehead. What was going on between her and the banker?

"Anything I can do to help?" Elizabeth's words seemed to snap Kat from her thoughts.

"No. Certainly not." Kat turned to Daniel. "I'm certain you can manage on your own this afternoon. The house is always open—come and go as you please." She watched him, and waited. For what, he didn't know. She turned away from his gaze.

What was the connection between Kat and his primary suspect, Chad Filcher? Daniel's job was to discover what that connection might be, and to determine the depth of Kat's involvement in the criminal activities.

Kat would never have come under suspicion except the investigator before

Daniel, who'd done the preliminary sur-
veillance on Filcher, noticed a change.
Subtle, but a change. The change had been
Kat. She'd spent a large amount of time
at the bank with Filcher the past month.
Did that mean there were grounds to believe she was involved in this mess?

Forget objectivity. Daniel hoped a connection didn't exist. The woman with her
quirky ways was getting to him.

In a good way.

Kat studied Daniel's expression, hoping to
discern his reaction. The meeting between
Daniel and Chad had been unexpected, but
Daniel's attention had definitely sharpened
when she'd introduced the two men. The
bank president and the man with a list of
robbed banks in his pocket. That didn't
prove a thing, and it didn't explain the list
from his pocket.

Kat walked to Elizabeth and pressed a
kiss to her delicate cheek. ''Take your

time finishing. I'll see you later today. Elizabeth leaned closer to Kat's ear. "I like Daniel. Better snatch him up before I do."

Kat glanced sideways to see if Daniel had overheard the whispered words. But he stood at the sink rinsing his cup. The running water covered the quiet conversation with Elizabeth.

"I'm not looking for a man," Kat answered her friend.

Elizabeth nodded knowingly. "That's usually when you'll find one."

Daniel turned to look at Kat with warmth in his eyes. Kat averted her gaze to the floor. If she didn't look at him, her body couldn't respond. Wishful thinking. Slow heat curled through her body and set a rushing sound loose in her ears. The man was too potent. Too real.

Kat escaped to the front parlor to prepare for her visitors. Anything to keep her mind off the man in the kitchen. Plumping a sofa pillow with unnecessary force, Kat thought ahead to the meeting with Chad. Would he have news? Was he any closer to discovering the missing account?

Despite her efforts, Daniel forced himself into her thoughts with all of the finesse of a bull elk. Could a man who reminded her of a television good guy be a felon in real life?

For reasons she didn't want to analyze, Kat hoped not.

Daniel lounged in the library adjoining the parlor and worked at his laptop. From this position, he was able to catch glimpses of Kat as she hurried through the house. All in the line of duty, of course. It helped that she was easy on the eyes.

The lunch crowd lingered over tea and scones, chatting and laughing with their charming hostess. Kat's laughter teased him.

Researching Kat had turned up only one significant development—a financial bind. Final payment on her business loomed at the bank where Chad Filcher worked. Was the deadline enough to push Kat into illegal involvement with a gang of bank robbers? Or, to cover for someone who might be involved?

Daniel watched Kat mingle with the guests. A warm smile put each guest at ease. Kat's easy conversational manner encouraged each person to share what was happening in their families and in their lives.

As Kat leaned to freshen a cup of tea, Daniel focused on the curve of calf above her short black boots. Only three inches of skin were exposed between the top of the boots and the bottom of the skirt, yet he felt the rush of heat in his face. The outfit she wore accentuated every feminine curve and hollow. She wasn't making it easy to keep his mind on business when every caveman instinct in him responded to her sensuality and spirit.

Daniel rubbed his bruised forehead. Looks could be deceiving. It was his job to find out just how deceiving.

"Oh, honey. Why didn't you come by?" Kat wrapped an arm about the shoulders of a slight, silver-haired woman who dabbed at the corner of her eyes with an embroidered handkerchief. "I don't care what time it is, Estelle, I'll find a tea to help with your aching joints."

The woman smiled up at Kat. "I know you would, Katherine. You are too good to me. Your aunt would be so proud."

Daniel watched Kat still the trembling in her lower lip by gently pulling it between her teeth. "Thank you. But promise me you'll come to me next time the discomfort keeps you from sleeping. How will you do story hour for the children at the library if you end up sick? They would miss you terribly." After a moment she gave the woman a small hug and moved to the next table.

The softness Kat's words brought to the woman's eyes with her softly spoken words was clear. With simple words she'd let this lady know someone cared and that her reading to children was important. It appeared to give the woman purpose.

How did Kat seem to know what each person needed to hear?

Finally, the visitors slipped away one by one. Kat peeked into the library to offer a quick goodbye when she left to meet with Filcher.

Daniel waited five minutes longer to be certain the house remained empty. Silence settled onto the old place as floorboards creaked and groaned. He snapped his computer shut and stood.

Glancing at the clock perched on the mantel, he planned his itinerary. First, Kat's bedroom. He walked down the hall and pushed her bedroom door open—a growl sounded behind him. He froze. Buster.

"Good dog." Daniel turned and extended his hand. The dog pointed his nose in the air and stalked off. Daniel sighed in relief. Obstacle one encountered and conquered.

He slipped inside and looked around. The room reflected Kat—soft and womanly, a combination of traditional woman and flower child.

A pang of guilt caught him square in the gut. Without a search warrant or badge, things weren't exactly on the right side of the books, but since he wasn't a lawman he'd use whatever means necessary. He needed to crack this case wide open and his employer allowed, no required, a certain amount of leeway. In this instance it was better to beg forgiveness than ask permission.

Daniel glanced around the room and decided the dresser was the place to start.

He slid the top drawer open. Lace and silk greeted him and the scent of lavender rose from inside. He'd pegged Kat for the cotton, Earth Mother variety of undergarments.

Stimulating surprise.

Daniel placed his hands in the frothy contents and ran his fingers under the panties and bras, along the sides of the drawer. No slip of paper, secret journal filled with confessions, or videotape of the heists. Had he really expected to locate evidence that easily?

Daniel removed his hands from Kat's sexy clothing, but a sheer bra snagged on the roughened edge of a fingernail. He held it in front of him and tried to remove it without damaging the delicate fabric.

He glanced at the window. The blood froze in his veins. Kat's bedroom window faced the house next door. Directly into a window where Elizabeth sat staring at him. Arms perched on the sill, she looked into his face and smiled.

Her voice carried on the crisp fall air. ''I'm afraid it's not your size, dear.''

CHAPTER THREE

DANIEL fumbled with the bra and tossed it back into the drawer. He crossed to the window while his mind furiously raced to devise a plausible excuse for fondling Kat's bra.

Who was he kidding? There was no explanation that wouldn't sound loony.

Time for the showdown.

Daniel leaned out of the window and faced Elizabeth. ''How are your knees feeling?''

''Better. What a sweet boy you are to ask. Shows you were raised properly.''

''I'll thank Mom next time I call. About the drawer—''

''Are you planning to prance about in Kat's things?''

Daniel blinked, caught off guard by the odd question. ''Hell, no.''

''Do you mean Kat any harm?''

''Not if I can avoid it.'' Daniel answered honestly.

''Well then, I believe that's about all we need to say on the subject.''

''You're sure?'' Daniel tried to keep his mouth from gaping like an addle-headed goat. Where else would he encounter a woman who didn't care he'd been rummaging in someone's dresser drawer and wearing underwear on his finger?

Elizabeth straightened in her chair. ''I just have one request.''

Here it comes—the blackmail. ''Yeah?''

''You and Kat name your first daughter after me.'' Having delivered that bombshell, she lowered the shade.

Daniel stared at the covered window and listened to Elizabeth's laughter. If his reputation hadn't been at stake, he'd high-tail it out of town right now. No way was he going to be able to sort out this mess without losing his mind.

A car engine sounded somewhere behind the house. Daniel stood and looked backward—the drawer hung open. He was losing his touch in his old age.

Old age. At thirty-three, Daniel felt ancient. Ten years working to expose those who would defraud the insurance industry pulled something out of a person. That was the reason he was losing impartiality on this assignment. Kat was a breath of fresh air, a mixture of fun and spontaneity rolled into one enticing package. The truth was, Daniel didn't want her to be involved with a criminal, even remotely.

He shut the drawer with more force than necessary and left the room. Stopping in the hall, he listened for sounds that would indicate Kat's return. There was only silence.

Where was the maddening woman? Why was her meeting with Filcher taking so long?

Most importantly, why did he care? For the sake of the investigation...or because of the nasty green monster stirring in his gut?

Kat tried to hide the yawn that sneaked out as Chad droned on about nothing. *Is the man ever going to shut up?* If he'd offered anything encouraging in the search for her aunt's money, Kat would have been happy to listen for days. As it was, he'd been spouting phony platitudes for over an hour.

Enough was enough.

Kat leaned forward in the concrete hard chair. Her butt cheeks were numb, had been for over twenty minutes. This was getting her nowhere, while at home, a gorgeous man waited.

Kat sighed. What a joke. Daniel West might be dreamy, but he was off limits. Even without his possible felonious involvement, Kat was focused on saving her business. Her great-aunt's legacy. She didn't have time for distractions.

"Chad."

He continued talking, obviously entranced by his own voice.

Kat spoke louder. "Chad?"

"Yes, Kat?" Chad leaned forward, all pompous concern. "Would you like me to repeat something?"

"No! I mean, no thank you," Kat said, "I'm sorry to interrupt when you've been so generous with your time, but I need to get home and prepare high tea."

Chad stood and moved from behind his mahogany desk. "Of course. How thoughtless of me to forget. Let me walk you out."

He was going to touch her. Kat's skin tightened in dread, as it always did when he reached toward her.

Chad grasped her hand between his soft, cool palms. ''Now, don't hesitate to call if you need *anything*. And, rest assured, I'll be working tirelessly to locate your stray account. We'll get through this.''

Kat smiled weakly. The sickening litany did not improve with repetition. She was tired of empty words. She wanted action. Darn it, she needed the money for her mortgage.

''Thank you. I'll remember.'' Kat tugged on her imprisoned arm.

Taking it as a sign of encouragement, Chad leaned closer. She averted her face in time and his dry lips grazed her cheek. It was too close for comfort.

Kat stepped backward to escape further contact. ''Goodbye.''

Chad flashed a practiced smile filled with capped teeth. The same smile focused on another woman might have elicited a quickened heartbeat. On Kat, it was wasted.

Stepping outside into the afternoon sunshine, Kat drew a breath of fresh, mountain air. Why did she always leave meetings with Chad feeling unclean? Half of the eligible women in Sugar Gulch were pursuing the man. Kat admitted to herself he was a catch. With his model looks and smooth manner, Chad fulfilled the requirements of a dream man for most women.

Just not for her.

She set off at a brisk pace—home was only three blocks away. Kat's steps faltered when an image of *her* dream man flashed through her mind.

Daniel West. No way—no how. The man was trouble. Rough, sexy, and seductive he might be, but Kat wasn't interested. She had too many responsibilities to focus her energy elsewhere.

So why did the thought of cornering

him in a secluded location cause her to break out in shivers of excitement?

Kat quickened her pace.

Three-thirty. The kitchen clock ticked on. Kat had been gone for over ninety minutes. Sixty minutes of which he'd used to search the rest of the house. Something was wrong. Daniel refused to pace the kitchen one more time. Instead, he reached for the doorknob.

The door opened inward before he touched it and banged his nose. ''Ouch!''

Kat peeked around the door. ''Don't tell me I injured you again.''

''My fault.'' Daniel glanced at his fingers. ''Look,'' he held his fingers up, ''no blood.''

Scampering claws on linoleum alerted Daniel to approaching trouble. He stepped back as Buster dashed past him. The dog flopped onto its back at Kat's feet. She kneeled on the floor and rubbed the belly offered by the idiot dog.

"That's my good boy. Did you miss me?" Kat stroked the sensitive skin on Buster's stomach as the dog whined in pleasure.

Daniel wondered if Kat would offer him the same treatment if he lay on the floor and wiggled. He shook his head ruefully. It would only happen in his out-of-control fantasies.

Kat gave Buster one last pat and stood. "How did your research go?"

"I admit to being lazy today. Only researched what my laptop could find." Daniel watched Kat cross the room. The sway of her hips derailed his train of thought.

"Well, we all need down days. Plus, just being here you're absorbing historical vibes." Kat rummaged in cabinets and placed items on the counter. "I serve high tea at six. It's a cold supper, but it's filling."

"Do you ever take time off?" Daniel leaned a hip against the counter and watched her gather items from various cabinets.

"Not often—running a business is a lot of work. Especially one that serves three meals a day and offers overnight accommodations." Kat paused and faced him. "I don't mean to sound ungrateful. The tearoom is my life and I love it. But sometimes I wish…"

"What do you wish?"

Kat shook her head and looked embarrassed. She returned to her busywork. "Nothing. I have everything I need. Or I hope to."

Daniel jerked upright. How was she getting "everything" she needed? With stolen money? "I forgot to ask how your meeting with the banker went."

"Not well."

"Too bad. Anything I can help with?" Daniel stared at Kat's profile and willed her to confide in him.

Sure. She'd known him less than twenty-four hours and she was going to spill her life story. *Wake up to reality, West.*

"Not unless you can locate missing money?"

Daniel snorted and covered it with a cough. Kat stared at him with an odd expression in her wide, green eyes. He needed to be more careful.

"I'm afraid my skills lie in the written word. Numbers aren't my strength," Daniel hedged.

Disappointment showed in Kat's eyes before she turned away. Daniel hated putting it there. She averted her gaze and opened the door to the pantry and flipped a switch inside. Nothing happened.

"Blast!" She stepped into the dark closet.

Daniel moved closer. He'd noticed the cavernous area during his speedy search of the house. ''Careful—'' A crash interrupted his warning. ''Are you all right?''

''Sure, if you don't count a bruised shin.'' Kat's voice faded into indecipherable muttering.

Daniel extended his arm and eased into the dark space. Why the heck did they make pantries so large back then?

''What are we looking for?'' Daniel said into the darkness.

''Honey straws,'' Kat answered from a step away.

''Honey straws?''

''To stir into the tea. Some of my regulars count on them to be on the tables.'' Kat shuffled to the left. ''Ah, they're here, right above my head.''

Daniel stepped toward the sound of her voice, her body a dim shadow in the faint light.

Distraction and temptation never looked so good.

*   *   *

Kat's breath caught in her throat. Daniel's body pressed close to hers as he reached for the elusive canister. All of her earlier forbidden fantasies about being alone in a secluded corner with this man flared to life.

Kat groaned aloud.

"What's wrong?" Daniel's warm breath brushed the top of her head.

"Stubbed my toe." She kicked the floor softly so the statement wouldn't be an outright lie.

Daniel grunted a reply and resumed his search of the upper shelf. Warmth drifted around her and with it, a familiar tug. Kat closed her eyes and absorbed the sensations. Images of her great-aunt and Elizabeth flitted through her mind, the lack of romance in their lives and the lonely golden years filled with regrets and dreams unfulfilled.

Just once, Kat wanted to experience the rush of doing something totally out of character. To skirt the edges of conventional society. Be naughty.

Before common sense could intrude on her rebellious moment, Kat reached into the darkness and touched what she'd fantasized about all day.

Daniel started and cleared his throat. Kat froze, horrified she'd actually played out her daydream as her open hand gripped one of Daniel's tight buttocks. *Hmm…even better than I imagined.*

She couldn't move or breathe. There was probably some law she was breaking by groping a guest in the pantry. Especially when the guest might be a crook. Maybe she'd claim to think his buttock was a melon. Right.

Just as she regained enough control to pull away, Kat felt Daniel move closer. Her back pressed against the shelves. Time seemed suspended and the world outside the pantry didn't exist.

Daniel's large, rough hand cupped her chin and his thumb brushed her lower lip.

Kat couldn't see his face clearly, but she sensed the desire emanating from his skin. ''Oh, my...''

Daniel swallowed her breathless words with his mouth. He bypassed tentative kisses for openmouthed exploration as his tongue slipped between her lips. Kat stopped thinking about the right or wrong of the situation and surrendered as Daniel's hands slipped behind her back and pulled her closer. She strained upward—eager to taste more of the mouth that was driving her beyond coherent thought. Her hands gripped the shirt straining against his shoulders.

Self-control was a distant annoyance.

Kat let her head fall back, exposing her neck to the gentle path taken by his mouth. The heat of his lips released the tightness coiled within her chest. She wanted more.

Kat hesitated, aware of the message she would send if they continued.

Daniel leaned down and ran his tongue across her lower lip. ''Kat?''

The whispered word blew across her mouth and she was lost...lost in a world of newly discovered passion. Newly discovered sensations. Why did this feel so right?

Kat shuddered as the enjoyable feelings washed over her.

''You make me want to forget who I am.''

Daniel's raw, honest words ignited an echoed yearning within Kat. Slipping her hands behind his head, she twined her fingers in Daniel's thick hair and pulled his lips over hers.

''Kat?'' A voice called from outside the pantry.

She ignored the voice of her conscience and enjoyed Daniel's mouth.

"Kat, dear, are you here?" Elizabeth's voice crashed into Kat's fogged mind.

Buster set up frenzied barking as he pushed the door to the pantry open. Kat winced. If she didn't do something, Buster would make use of his doggy incisors on Daniel's leg.

Kat rested her forehead against Daniel's muscled chest and prepared for ultimate humiliation. "Buster, hush."

Elizabeth appeared in the doorway. "What are you doing in there, Kat? Why isn't the light on?" She squinted at them.

Daniel spoke. "The light burned out. I was helping Kat find her honey."

Lame. Lame. Lame. Kat chanted the word over and over in her head. Elizabeth wasn't an idiot. *I'll never live this down.*

"Oh, how nice of you, Daniel. What a gentleman." Elizabeth took a step backward. "I'll just take Buster back out for a walk before I help you with dinner preparations, Kat."

The elderly woman called Buster and pushed the pantry door closed.

Kat gaped at the place where her friend had stood moments before. In the darkness she couldn't even see Daniel's chest under her hand.

Her hand. She yanked her appendage back as though his skin scorched it through Daniel's shirt. Illusion was gone and reality had come back with a bark and a growl. How could she face Daniel after behaving like a lunatic?

''Kat?''

She didn't answer him, couldn't answer him. Kat had grabbed for adventure and excitement with both hands, literally, and she wasn't prepared to face the conse-quences.

Daniel placed his hands on her shoul-ders. ''This isn't finished.''

''Yes, it is. I'm sorry.'' She drew a shuddering breath. ''I behaved like a...a harlot.''

"You're behaving like a woman with desires." Daniel moved closer. "There's no shame in that." His mouth softly touched hers.

Kat kept her lips compressed for all of two seconds. With a groan, she returned his kiss. Regrets could be faced later.

Kat kissed her outlaw like there was no tomorrow. And enjoyed it shamelessly.

CHAPTER FOUR

DANIEL stared up through the bare branches of the aspen tree. Its skeletal arms reached for the moon—an unattainable goal, like any relationship he might want with Kat.

He kicked at the leaves piled beneath the tree. Daniel knew better than to cross the line with someone involved in a case.

Hadn't the call with his supervisor earlier that afternoon been enough to remind Daniel why he was here? Evidently not. Information had been discovered that led Global to believe more strongly than ever that the heists were manipulated from inside the First National Bank hierarchy.

Evidently, money delivery schedules had been known and security codes for each branch had been utilized in the holdups. Now all Daniel had to do was draw the connection between what he suspected of Filcher and his involvement. Simple. Except for the unexpected glitch of being attracted to a woman who might be involved in the robberies. A circle is what the situation was...a convoluted circle with sharp corners.

He glanced toward the house where golden light beckoned through the windows. Kat was in there. Warm, giving, sexy, spontaneous, and off limits. His personal code demanded he not allow a repeat of the incident in the pantry.

Incident. Such a cold, clinical word for the most mind-blowing kisses he'd ever experienced. Surprise had quickly turned to desire when Kat had reached for him.

Maybe she was using physical distraction to knock him off balance and keep his mind off his job. Did Kat suspect why he was in Sugar Gulch? Why else did she watch him so closely?

Filcher might have warned Kat to be wary of strangers, fearing the authorities were getting closer to his operation. The man had covered his tracks well. He'd been under suspicion for several weeks before the connection to Kat was noticed.

Daniel slammed the trunk of the tree with his open palm and welcomed the sting. By allowing himself to become distracted, it was becoming difficult to maintain his objectivity and perspective.

Passion he could live with. It was the stirring of deeper feelings that worried him. He didn't want a relationship and certainly didn't need one.

So, why did the thought of Kat being linked to a criminal bother him? Why did it trouble him to think of leaving Sugar Gulch and never looking back?

To sum up his first twenty-four hours in town, Daniel was hot, bothered, and no closer to solving the case than when he'd arrived.

The back door squeaked open and Kat stepped into the yard. She used one hand to hold the hem of her robe above the damp grass, and an iron skillet in the other hand. Of course—bacon grease for the chrysanthemums.

Daniel eased back against the tree and blended into the shadows.

Kat's voice drifted to him while she spoiled the vegetation.

"Honest, Aunt Bernice, you'd have done the same thing. Well, maybe not exactly the same, but you'd have been tempted."

Daniel grinned. Kat was strange, but in a good way—if there was such a thing. He hadn't believed she really talked to her dead aunt. His ears tuned in when her voice continued.

"I know, I know."

What did Kat know? A one-sided conversation wasn't the easiest to follow.

"But he's funny, handsome as sin, and brave enough to try my tea."

Was she raving about Filcher?

"I know he's only been here little more than a day..."

Daniel nearly slapped a high five on the tree bark. *Yes! I'm getting to her.* He frowned. *Why am I so excited? This is the last thing I need. Isn't it?*

"And the pantry. I can't believe I actually grabbed his bottom. What was I thinking?"

Daniel's fondled cheek tightened in remembrance.

"You'd have thought I was the town tart, instead of the woman voted most likely to shun romance. Of course, I'm not certain if what we did constituted romance or plain old lust." Kat scraped the last of the grease out of the pan. "Well, I'll make sure it doesn't happen again. I can resist Daniel West's charms."

Daniel watched Kat straighten her shoulders before she stepped inside the house. Kat had tossed a challenge in his face, whether she knew it or not.

The next move was his. Daniel smiled and wondered if he could lure her into the pantry again.

Whistling under his breath, Daniel set off on a walk around the block.

Kat glanced at the clock. Again. Only six minutes since the last time she'd checked. Where the devil was Daniel? He'd stepped outside after high tea and two hours later there was still no sign of him. Not that she really cared, but he was her guest. She was responsible for him.

Yeah, right. How many guests had she pictured naked while she served them dinner? Zero. Until Daniel arrived.

The man infuriated her. His gaze had followed her all evening, letting her know he remembered the interlude in the pantry.

Kat tingled every time she allowed her mind to drift back to those moments.

How can a man I've just met have this effect on my life and my libido?

Kat was so careful to keep everything about her life completely under control. To have this out of control feeling about a man was throwing her off track.

No sense losing sleep over him. Daniel was a big boy and could take care of himself.

Daniel waited until the kitchen went dark. The walk he'd taken had only eaten up a few minutes and checking the pistol he was licensed to carry and kept locked in the car trunk took less than five more. Now his legs were cramped from sitting in the decrepit lawn chair for over an hour.

He shook his head. It was a good thing he'd opted not to carry his gun the night before. Kat would have discovered it when she'd helped him into her house. Surprise was still on his side—he hoped.

Daniel didn't imagine Filcher knew who he was, but things felt…strange. Kat watched him. Her gaze rarely left him when they were in the same room. Daniel wanted to believe it was his body that attracted her attention, but it could be his profession. Maybe she'd discovered he was an insurance investigator.

There was no way to know for sure. And that made things dangerous.

The light in Kat's room came on and her silhouette passed in front of the window twice before she pulled the shade. Too late. Daniel had glimpsed the pure white nightgown, the nightgown that displayed her curves each time she moved in front of the lamp.

He needed to focus on his past mistakes and the reasons to avoid involvement with Kat.

First, possible involvement with a criminal. Second, she was a key figure in his current assignment. Third, and most importantly, he'd never allow a woman power over him again.

Daniel opened the back door and slipped inside. Thank goodness, his mental list was the equivalent of a cold shower. Sleep would come easier now.

Hand still on the knob, he stopped and stared at Kat standing in front of the stove. She gripped a steaming kettle with an oven mitt and candlelight gave her gown the consistency of tissue paper. He cleared his throat.

Kat jumped. ''I didn't hear you come in.''

''I know.'' White, cotton nightgowns were his new favorite.

''Would you like some tea? I couldn't sleep, so I thought I'd better have a special blend.'' Looking embarrassed, Kat turned back to her task.

Daniel glanced at the three candles burning on the counter.

Kat glanced over her shoulder and noticed where his gaze focused.

"Aroma therapy. Sage and lavender candles. Thought it might help me to sleep." Kat stirred her tea, then wiped her palms on her gown. Her gaze flew to his face as she remembered what she wore. "Oh…"

Daniel took pity at the shocked expression on her readable face. "Nice gown. I'll pass on the tea tonight. Thanks."

Kat's soft good-night followed him down the hallway to his room.

Damn, he needed a cold shower again.

A light tap on the glass of the kitchen door caught Kat's attention.

Now what? Peering through the lace curtains, she saw Elizabeth smiling and waving.

Kat pulled the door open. ''What are you doing out at this time of night?''

''The same as you, dear.'' Elizabeth shrugged out of her wool coat and settled into a chair.

''You couldn't sleep?''

''I meant your other reason for being up. Daniel came in late this evening.'' Her face creased into a smile.

Kat pretended indifference. ''I hadn't noticed.''

Elizabeth chuckled. ''Now, Kat, lie to yourself if you must, but you know your face can't keep a secret. That man is getting to you.''

Kat turned back to the stove and ignored the comments. What could she say? It was true. ''What tea can I make for you?''

''Do you have any Passion Flower made up?''

Kat glanced at her friend.

"Just tea—I wasn't making reference to the interlude in the pantry."

"Oh, you're incorrigible. Nothing happened." Kat spun away, but she knew Elizabeth had seen the truth in her eyes.

"I imagine he's a good kisser."

Kat handed the cup to her friend, curiosity piqued. "Why do you say that?"

Elizabeth sipped and ignored the question. "Mmm…delicious. Just what I need to soothe my nerves."

"You were going to tell me why you thought Daniel would be a good kisser."

"I was? Of course." She set her cup on the table and reached out to gently cradle Kat's hands in her own. "His full lips. Not so pretty that they make him look foppish, but just full enough to tempt even the most prudish girl."

Kat stared and her mouth sagged in surprise. Elizabeth never ceased to throw something unexpected into the mixture.

"Did you forget I was young once? Many is the time your aunt and I would compare notes on how one man or another kissed." Elizabeth giggled. "Stop gaping at me. Kissing was around in those days and it was as enjoyable then for me as it appeared to be for you today."

Kat leaned forward and wrapped her arms around Elizabeth. "Forgive me for being so narrow-minded. But it won't work for Daniel and me. He will be leaving when he finishes his story." She sat back in her chair and gazed fondly at her friend.

"Nonsense. If you'd come out of your self-imposed love exile, it just might. After all, he likes your undergarments." She sipped her tea.

Kat straightened. "What do you mean he likes my undergarments?" Surely she'd misheard her friend.

"The way he was fondling the bras in your drawer, there's no doubt."

"Wait a minute." Kat shook her head. Sometimes things became fuddled in her friend's mind. "What are you talking about?"

Elizabeth glanced toward the hallway door and lowered her voice. "It was while you were at the bank. But I promised Daniel I wouldn't mention it. I do so hate to go back on my word. I truly didn't mean to spill the proverbial beans."

Kat felt the blood drain from her head and focused on the steam swirling from her cup. Daniel *had* to be a criminal. Why else would he rummage through her things? What could he be looking for in her home?

No way would she let the man use her to rob the Sugar Gulch bank. No wonder he was interested in how her meeting with Chad had gone. Daniel was here to case the bank and learn its routines. Then he'd hit it and disappear, never to be seen in these parts again.

Kat wished the robbery part bothered her as much as the disappearing part. Her chin angled upward as she decided on a course of action. It might be the wrong move, but it was better than sitting around wringing her hands like a helpless ninny.

Daniel West was going to wish he'd never heard of the Naked Moon Tearoom, much less Kat Bennett.

She patted Elizabeth's hand. "I have a problem, love. And I'm going to need your help to work it out."

Her friends eyes lit up. "I do enjoy a quandary."

Taking a breath, Kat continued. "Daniel and I can't get involved because he's planning to rob the bank."

Elizabeth's lips formed a perfect circle. "Nonsense. If he's a bank robber, I'm a beauty queen."

"I wish it wasn't true, but I have proof."

"What kind of proof?"

"I found a list in his pants."

Elizabeth tilted her head and smiled. "What were you doing in his pants, dear?"

"Not like that. I washed his jeans last night and the list fell out of his pocket. It's a list of all the banks in this part of the state that have been robbed in that string of heists."

"Maybe there is another, perfectly reasonable, explanation for that list."

"It isn't only that. He acts odd, watches me all the time, questioned me about the meeting with Chad. And he was lurking outside last night."

"Well, of course he watches you. Don't you look in the mirror? Most of the young men in town watch you. Not that you'd ever notice." Elizabeth sighed. "Bernice and I did you a great injustice. It's no wonder your head is only on this business—we let you take over at much too tender an age."

"Nonsense." Kat stood. "Let me get you a fresh cup of tea. I'm afraid I've cancelled all the benefit of the first one." She talked while she worked. "You and Bernice did a stupendous job. I'm simply not interested in a romantic relationship right now."

"But I think a romantic relationship is interested in you." The kind woman smiled. "You can't do anything about fate, except to accept it graciously."

"It's safe to say that I'm not going to have a relationship with a suspected felon."

"We'll see. I don't believe for a second Daniel is a criminal. He doesn't have the look."

Kat wanted to have the same conviction, but was afraid of finding out Daniel actually was a criminal. She placed the fresh tea on the table and faced the inevitable. Elizabeth was smitten with Daniel. "We'll need to do some discreet investigating. Ask questions without attracting a lot of attention.''

''No problem. I have connections you wouldn't believe.''

Kat smiled. ''Good. Let's plan on starting first thing in the morning. And remember, not a word to Daniel.''

''You can count on me. I know how to keep a secret.''

The library didn't open until ten. Kat killed time by drying fresh tea leaves as Daniel lingered over breakfast. The weight of his intense gaze kept her on edge and made it impossible to concentrate. And her traitorous body responded to him every second.

Daniel finally left the house, mentioning that a visit to the museum was on his agenda for the day. She hoped his absence from the house would relieve the sensual tension surging through her in waves.

His absence did offer an opportunity to look through Daniel's things.

Kat watched through the living room window until he disappeared from sight. She peeked around the door and paused. Touching someone else's possessions stuck in her throat like a lemon wedge.

The top drawer revealed his underwear. Not the plain white briefs she'd expected, but low-cut, multicolored creations. Kat pulled one out and held it up, turning it back and forth. Bad idea. She squeezed her eyes shut in an attempt to stem the visual images flying through her mind.

It was no use. Why couldn't the man have boring underwear? It would make things a lot easier.

Kat carefully refolded the briefs and put them away. The rest of Daniel's clothing offered no help at all. Faded jeans and worn sweatshirts did not a felon make.

The door shut quietly as she stepped into the hall. Kat glanced at her watch—

it was time to meet Elizabeth and head to the library. Her friend had guaranteed a contact in the reference section. Kat sighed. It couldn't hurt to try.

Slipping her arms into the sleeves of her corduroy jacket, Kat noticed Elizabeth waiting on the front walk, punctual as ever.

Bright autumn sunshine greeted Kat as she stepped outside. Sunglasses helped cut the glare. ''Morning. Are you sure you want to get involved in this?''

''Try to stop me. It's about time something happened in this town.''

Kat slipped Elizabeth's hand into the crook of her elbow as they set off at a leisurely pace. She could have made better time on her own, but Kat enjoyed the company.

''Are you certain your friend will be at the library?'' Kat asked.

''Oh, yes. She's been volunteering in the reference department for twelve years now. Rarely misses a day. Will you admit you were wrong if we clear Daniel's name?''

The quick change in subject threw Kat for only a moment. ''Elizabeth, if I'm wrong, I'll sing show tunes in town square.'' She gently squeezed her friend's hand. ''I honestly hope I'm mistaken. Not that it changes the fact that Daniel and I are wrong for each other.''

''How so?''

''Well...he's so...uptight. Doesn't seem to believe in anything he doesn't have a statistic on.''

''So? Many perfectly happy couples are complete opposites.'' Elizabeth stopped and peered at her above the rim of her bifocals. ''Like your parents. For goodness' sake, your father was a law professor and your mother a belly dancer. And they always found each other fascinating.''

''I know. And that was great for them. But this is different. Daniel would tire of my oddities, as he believes them to be, and I'm not willing to move. I like living here.''

Kat pondered all of the reasons any type of involvement with Daniel was out of the question. They were too different, lived too far apart, not to mention his possible criminal status. They continued walking in silence until they reached the library.

Kat took a deep breath. ''Now remember, we have to be discreet. We don't want to draw attention to ourselves.''

''Don't you worry. I watch all those detective shows on television.'' Elizabeth tugged her oversize purse higher on her shoulder with a determined glint in her eyes.

Winding their way through the tables and stacks, Kat stayed back while Elizabeth approached the reference counter smiling warmly at her friend. ''Good morning, Wilma.''

Wilma cupped a hand behind her ear. ''Heh?''

''We need some information.'' Elizabeth spoke a tad louder.

Kat grimaced. This was not going well. Luckily no one seemed to be paying attention to them.

''I said, we need some information.'' Now, Elizabeth's voice was noticeable in the echoing room.

''On what?'' asked Wilma.

''Bank robberies.''

Several heads turned in their direction. Kat tried to catch Elizabeth's eye, but her friend was focused on Wilma.

''The ones in the news.''

''Why?'' Wilma's voice was nearly a shout.

''Kat here thinks she knows who the robber is,'' Elizabeth yelled.

Kat groaned as Elizabeth clamped a hand over her mouth and turned an apologetic gaze to her. It was too late—the damage was done. Thank goodness a weekday afternoon in the library wasn't a busy time.

"I think we'll try this another time," Kat said, tugging on Elizabeth's arm.

"Oh, my dear. I'm sorry. I forget how dreadfully hard of hearing Wilma is. And she's too stubborn to wear hearing aids."

"It's all right. Let's leave before we make things worse." Kat turned to lead the way down the nearest aisle but she stopped when she saw the man silhouetted against a nearby window. Daniel.

The look on his face told her he'd heard Elizabeth. As had half the county. It shouldn't have been a surprise to find him there, but it was.

Elizabeth elbowed her in the ribs, jarring her into action. Kat didn't want to face Daniel. She hurried to the entrance and bumped into the solid chest of a man entering the library.

Chad.

Oh, good. Was anyone left out of the drama?

Chad steadied her with a hand on her waist. ''Are you all right?''

Kat slipped past his arm and pulled the door open. ''Fine, thanks. Have to go.'' He'd hear everything from the gossips anyway, no sense wasting time filling him in on the juicy details of her humiliation.

A quick glance over her shoulder caused her to hasten her steps, as much as she could while helping Elizabeth. Daniel was headed their way and he looked grim. Grim, determined, and bewildered.

Kat stepped into the street and waved down the first cab that drove by.

Back at the house, Buster greeted them with his happy dance and sloppy licks.

''Not now, boy.'' Kat turned the dead bolt, wanting to avoid Daniel for as long as possible. She'd never used it before and it didn't make her feel any better. Only her tea could do that. A double dose to calm her and help her think clearly.

''Kat, don't overreact. You don't know that Daniel is responsible for the robberies.'' Elizabeth draped her sweater over a kitchen chair.

''We don't know he isn't. And he heard every word at the library.'' Kat turned the flame on under the kettle and paced.

''We'll deal with it when it comes up.''

Kat stopped pacing and rubbed her forehead. ''Okay, I need to think. What would a policeman do in this situation?''

Ha. Kat wasn't seasoned at anything other than running a tearoom—not exactly the skills required under the circumstances. She closed her eyes and took deep, cleansing breaths.

''He'd secure the perimeter.'' Daniel's voice stole Kat's breath.

Her eyes flew open. There he stood, inside the door, with Buster licking his hand. Why hadn't she remembered to bolt the back door? And where was her man-hating dog when she needed him?

Elizabeth calmly pulled three teacups from the cabinet. "Can I fix you something, Daniel?"

He answered without taking his gaze from Kat. "Do you have any of that gimbo?"

"You mean gingko?" Kat's voice was a whisper.

"That's the one."

"What…what are you doing back so early?" Kat swallowed, knowing the answer before he spoke.

"I finished at the museum and headed to the library to explore their archives. Overheard an interesting conversation between Elizabeth," Daniel smiled at the older woman, "and the reference counter woman."

"Oh." Kat gripped the back of a nearby chair.

Daniel stepped closer. ''I thought you might like to flesh out your bank robber theory with someone.''

''Oh.''

''You already said that.''

Kat looked to Elizabeth for help, but her friend was busy straining the loose tea into teacups. And Buster still licked Daniel's hand. *Rotten, traitor dog.*

Elizabeth turned and smiled at Kat and Daniel. ''Time for tea. Come sit down, both of you.''

The whole world seemed a little mad. Kat now knew how Alice felt when she'd fallen down the rabbit's hole. Didn't anyone realize what was going on? The man she feared was a criminal had them cornered—trapped like frightened animals. Didn't her friend realize the dangerous situation they were in?

While she stared incredulously at Elizabeth, a large hand clamped down on Kat's shoulder. Daniel's hand.

Oh, no. He wasn't going to silence *her*.

Kat spun and ground her heel into his foot while thrusting her elbow into his chin.

CHAPTER FIVE

DANIEL'S head jerked back and he grunted in stunned surprise. He hadn't expected Kat to take direct confrontational physical action.

You'd think I'd know better. She'd done it that first night, chances had to be over seventy-eight percent that she'd do the same if cornered.

Kat stood in front of Elizabeth, shielding her with her body, her fists raised in poor imitation of a boxer's stance. Fire was in her eyes, and fear.

Daniel rubbed his chin, thinking ruefully that the ache in his jaw overshadowed the lump on his forehead. He stared at the women, one in a parody of a fighter's pose, the other smiling a secre-

tive smile. Buster stood in the midst of them all, whining.

Elizabeth broke the silence. "For heaven's sake, Daniel. Tell the poor girl you're not the bank robber before she inflicts another injury to your face."

Daniel stared at Kat. "The what? You think *I'm* the bank robber?"

Kat didn't back down. "Darned right I do."

"Why?"

"The list of banks I found in your pocket when I washed your pants, the way you were lurking around when you arrived, all your questions about the bank, and the way you watch me all the time. Need any more reasons?"

Daniel shook his head. "The list of banks is connected to my job, I didn't know what I was walking into the night I arrived, the questions were to test you, and I stare at you because you're sexy as hell."

Elizabeth clapped her hands with delight. "I told you, Kat."

Kat lowered her fists only a quarter of an inch. "What kind of a job ties you to the banks that were robbed?"

Daniel sighed. Judging from Kat's reaction, she wasn't involved with the robberies unless she was a great actress. But he knew her eyes would have betrayed her if she'd been anything less than totally honest.

He'd have to take a chance. "I'm working undercover, investigating the robberies for the company that insures the banks against loss not covered by the federal government. A lead in the case led me to Sugar Gulch." Daniel withheld facts Kat didn't need to know, and prepared to deliver his bombshell. "I believed you were somehow involved."

Kat's arms dropped to her sides. "Me? You are kidding? Right? And just where is all the money I supposedly stole?" Her rising anger brought color flaming to her face. "*If* I had the money, I wouldn't be on the verge of losing the Naked Moon."

Buster slunk out of the room. Daniel wanted to follow the mutt. "Now, Kat—"

"Don't you dare 'Now, Kat' me. And what was the pantry? A little in-depth research into my moral character?"

"If I remember correctly, *you* grabbed *me.*"

"You're no gentleman for bringing that up." Kat's gaze dropped to the floor.

Elizabeth stepped in. "That's not true. He asked about my bad knees and promised not to wear any of your undergarments."

Daniel laughed. "She's right—I did promise." He saw the struggle on Kat's face, the emotions chasing each other across her lovely features.

Kat finally smiled. A small smile, but it was there. "I want the details about what brought you to town, or who?"

Daniel waited for the women to sit before he pulled a chair out.

Kat's voice stopped him before his bottom touched the seat. "I'll need to see some identification."

Daniel pulled his wallet out and displayed his driver's license and a business card. Kat nodded.

Elizabeth held her hand out. "May I see that picture?"

Daniel handed her his wallet. "It's my family." Kat's face paled. "My mom, dad, and sisters."

Kat straightened. "Do you have…are you…married?"

"No, thank God. You won't see me making that mistake."

Elizabeth glanced up. "You don't believe in marriage?"

"It's fine for other people, but I won't change to make someone accept me."

"That's odd, Kat said something similar to me this morning on our way to the library."

Daniel cleared his throat. "That reminds me, what were you two doing at the library? And why?"

Kat answered in a defensive voice. "Investigating someone I thought was a felon. I didn't remember about Wilma's deafness until it was too late."

"Do you realize the danger you've put yourself, and Elizabeth, in?"

Kat glared at him. "What do you mean?"

"You announced to anyone within hearing that you know who robbed the banks."

Kat's brow wrinkled. "But I don't, since it's not you."

"Ah, but the real criminal doesn't know that. And the way news travels in small towns, that person will have heard about the incident in the library by lunchtime."

Kat looked at her watch. "Lunchtime! I only have an hour until the Ladies Book Club arrives for lunch."

Elizabeth stood. "We'll help you." She pierced Daniel with her gaze. "Won't we, dear?"

Daniel smiled. The woman might look fragile, but she had a cast-iron will. "Yes, ma'am."

Between the three of them, they assembled enough cucumber and watercress sandwiches to feed the herd of guests.

Daniel stared at the tiny, meatless, sandwiches. "People actually eat these? Where's the roast beef or ham? And why are they so small?" He picked one up and sniffed it.

Kat arranged crumpets and scones on glass platters. "I try to serve a variety of dishes, basing most on traditional tea delicacies served in different countries."

"Oh." Daniel nibbled a corner of the sandwich. The creamy sauce had a zing to it. He ate the rest in one bite. "Not bad. With all this new vocabulary I'm learning, maybe I'll write a book."

Elizabeth turned from the pile of fresh fruit she was washing. ''Then you really are a writer?''

''No, I'm really an insurance investigator. But I have had an article or two published.'' Daniel busied himself by washing the stack of dirty dishes.

Kat stared at him. ''Have you always wanted to do investigative work?''

Daniel glanced up from the soapy water to find both women staring at him as though his answer mattered.

''Yeah, I think I have. My folks never understood it, but most of the time I didn't either. Just something I was born to do, I suppose.'' Daniel watched Elizabeth shoot Kat an ''I told you so'' look. He'd never understand these two.

''You still haven't mentioned who you came to town to investigate, besides me.'' Kat's expression was that of an injured animal.

Daniel dried his hands and walked to Kat. He wanted to answer without lying *and* without jeopardizing his case. ''I didn't know you. There was no way to decide if you were involved or not until I came here.'' Daniel put a finger under her chin and gently encouraged her to look at him. ''I'm sorry.''

Kat stared into his eyes for endless seconds. Everything else faded and the memory of her pliant lips beneath his tugged at him. Her lips trembled and he leaned toward her. Only a breath separated their mouths when her eyes widened and she stepped backward.

Elizabeth was gone, singing from somewhere in the front of the house.

Kat gripped both hands together and her knuckles shone white. ''I owe you an apology, too. I jumped to the wrong conclusions about you.'' She stepped around the table, seeming to need a barrier between them. ''Yesterday was a mistake and it can't happen again. After you're done with this case, you'll be gone. And I'm not a one-night stand kind of a woman.''

Daniel nodded. He didn't analyze why her confession made him feel better. After all, she was basically giving him the brush-off. If not for the desire he saw buried in the depths of her eyes, he might have moved on. But, right or wrong, good or bad, this woman was in his blood. And, damned if he didn't want to hear her moan against his mouth again.

Kat broke eye contact and turned away. ''I'm going to shower and change. Could you let Elizabeth know I'll be right out?'' She walked two steps before she turned again. ''Thank you for your help.''

Daniel saluted her with another small sandwich before popping it into his mouth as she vanished down the hall.

The little sandwiches grew on a fellow. Course, he'd die of starvation if he were expected to make an entire meal of them. Daniel rummaged through the refrigerator for some meat and cheese.

Maybe cucumber and watercress would add flavor to a *real* sandwich.

Kat stood while the water cascaded over her and tried to force all thoughts from her mind as the water slipped through her hair. With her eyes closed, an image of Daniel scrubbing her hair with his long fingers pushed its way into her conscience.

Double blast.

Kat meant it when she'd told Daniel they couldn't become involved. Unfortunately, her body hadn't received the message. Or it was simply ignoring it. A few stolen moments of passion did not make the beginnings of a relationship. But, if Kat had been attracted to Daniel while thinking he was a felon, it was doubly tempting knowing he was a decent law-abiding citizen.

Kat flipped the warm water spigot off and shivered while ice-cold water pummeled her. Get it out of your head, girl. Daniel was passing through, leaving town when he finished the investigation. What harm could a fling cause?

Plenty.

Dripping, Kat stepped onto the mat and rubbed herself dry. The last thing she needed was to be left with a broken heart if she fell for with Daniel. Heaven knew it was possible—she was halfway there already.

What if I never experience passion like this again? Would regrets mar her golden years? Wondering what might have been, if she'd only taken a chance and savored the moment?

Kat wiped a circular area on the fogged mirror and stared at her reflection, the image smudged and blurry. What was it going to be? An attempted seduction of

Daniel West or a lifetime filled with un-fulfilled dreams?

How do I know he even wants me? Memories of the moment she'd taken a chance in the pantry caused her body to tighten. He'd wanted her. She'd make him want her again.

The afternoon dragged as Kat passed through the book club's lunch in a daze. Questions were answered, jokes told, but she couldn't recall any of it afterwards. Daniel completely occupied her thoughts.

Enough.

Kat needed to focus on more important issues. Like how to avoid losing her busi-ness *and* her home. Replacing the last clean cup in the cupboard, Kat flipped the kitchen light off and let Buster out, fol-lowing him into the backyard. Twenty feet from the house, Buster planted his feet and snarled.

Kat glanced into the shadows. ''Who's there? Daniel?'' Buster howled and ran into the darkness on the side of the house. Frenzied barking was followed by a bellow of pain.

"Get off me, ignorant mongrel! Kat!" Chad called out. "Can you get this untrained beast off me?"

Kat rushed to find Chad clinging to the lowest branch of an aspen tree. Buster had his teeth clamped on the cuff of his trousers, shaking ruthlessly.

"Buster, come." Kat gave the two-toned whistle and the dog ran to her side. "He *is* trained, which is why you're up a tree." She tried to keep the laughter out of her voice. Where was her camera when she needed it? "You can come down."

Chad eyed Buster doubtfully. "Maybe you could lock him in the house."

"He's fine. Why in the world are you sneaking around in the dark anyway?"

Chad lowered himself to the ground and surveyed the damage to his pants. "I heard there was a commotion at the library today and I came by to make sure you were all right.''

His concern seemed sincere. ''Come on inside.'' Kat didn't want to prolong his visit, but her dog had treed the man like a squirrel, so she felt she owed him something.

Kat led the way into the kitchen and turned the small counter lamp on. She didn't want to be alone in the dark with the man. Buster remained next to her leg and tossed hostile looks in Chad's direction, which caused the nervous man to stay several feet away.

Chad sat on the chair farthest from Buster. ''What is going on, Kat? And how are you involved in a bank robbery investigation?''

Kat stayed next to the stove—the farthest point from Chad. ''I'm not, it was a misunderstanding.'' Something about the shrewd look in his gaze kept her from mentioning her former suspicions about

Daniel. Being undercover, Daniel wouldn't appreciate her revealing his true purpose for being in Sugar Gulch. ''Wilma wasn't wearing her hearing aid again. You know how difficult it can be to get a point across to her. Or a question.''

Chad nodded. ''So you really don't know anything about the robberies?''

''I wish. The reward might help me out of the fix I'm in.''

Kat finally moved to the table and sat across from Chad.

Chad reached across and gripped her hand. It wasn't a large enough table.

''I've told you I'll do anything I can to help. All you have to do is say the word,'' he said.

Buster growled and Kat resisted an urge to slip him a treat. She was beginning to understand what Chad might expect in return for his ''help.'' ''Thank you, Chad.'' Kat slid her hand free. ''I appreciate your offer, but it's important that I do this on my own.''

Chad straightened. ''Very well, but you know the offer stands.'' He stood. ''I'd better get home.''

Kat tried to hide her relief. ''Thanks for your concern.'' She opened the back door and stepped aside to let him pass.

''Good night, my dear.'' Chad used the opportunity of her position against the doorjamb to move closer.

Kat pulled her head back, and thumped it against the door. Chad placed his moist lips against her mouth for a fraction of a second, then he was gone. Buster stood with hackles raised, waiting for Kat's attack command.

''It's okay, boy.'' Kat wiped the back of her hand roughly across her mouth, trying to erase the awful feeling Chad's kiss left behind. *Why can't I lust after a respectable banker, instead of a hot-shot in-*

vestigator who'll be riding into the sunset before I can catch my breath?

Daniel stepped out of the shadows next to the trunk of the large aspen in the backyard. Kat froze. How long had he been there?

"You might try some antibacterial soap. Never know where his mouth's been." Daniel smiled and walked into the kitchen.

"You're quite the funny man. Are you still spying on me?" Kat slammed the door. It was childish but it made her feel better.

"Not at all. I was just getting home when I noticed the touching scene taking place on the back step. Didn't want to interrupt." Daniel turned a chair backward and straddled it.

Kat stared at the denim stretched taut over his thighs. Daniel noticed the direction of her gaze and smiled.

Kat forced herself to focus on his face. "Next time, interrupt. Please."

"Then you and banker boy aren't...intimate?" Daniel looked at his nails as Kat sputtered.

"What does that have to do with your investigation? Frankly, my personal life is none of your business." Kat's anger rose the more she fumed. "Just because you and I shared a bit of passion, doesn't give you a claim on me or a right to stick your nose into my life."

"I never said it did." Daniel stared at her as if she'd sprouted an extra eye in the middle of her forehead.

Kat cringed. She'd gone off like a woman possessed. What was she thinking? What would Daniel think of her? She took a step backward.

"I'm sorry, Daniel. The last couple of days have been...odd. But that's no excuse to attack you." Kat offered her hand. "Forgive me? Can we start over?"

Daniel stood. The scent of his cologne tantalized her.

He returned her handshake. "Forgiven." Daniel cocked an eyebrow. "I'm Daniel West, it's a pleasure to meet you."

Kat grinned. He was taking her words at face value. "Kat Bennett. Ditto."

Daniel didn't release her hand. Awareness raced up her arm and spread through her limbs.

Kat looked away. "I hope you'll enjoy your stay at the Naked Moon, Mr. West." Her words tumbled over each other in a frantic scramble to exit her mouth.

Daniel tugged on her hand. "I plan to. Rumor has it this place has a hell of a pantry."

Kat sucked air into her paralyzed lungs, unable to resist the steady pressure pulling her closer, nearer to her fantasies personified. She lifted her face to accept his kiss.

Buster pushed between them, nosing Daniel's free hand for attention. Kat jumped back. Buster's timing stunk, but it was for the best. She hadn't made up her mind about Daniel, didn't know if she could walk away if her emotions became entangled.

In that moment, Kat knew her heart was involved. Daniel had stolen it when she'd been looking elsewhere, taken it without a second thought. But he'd never know, because Kat wasn't going to risk heartbreak by telling him.

Besides, Daniel would never believe her. Mr. Feet-Solidly-on-the-Ground wouldn't understand that she'd felt a connection the moment they'd banged into each other. A sense that her search was over and she hadn't even know she'd been looking.

Elizabeth had warned her. Romance would find you when you weren't looking for it. When you least thought you needed it.

This was getting her nowhere. Kat turned toward the hallway. ''Please turn out the lights when you go to bed. I'll leave my door open so Buster can come in when he's ready.'' She didn't look at him while she spoke, afraid her eyes would reveal too much of her inner turmoil. ''Night.''

Daniel didn't answer and Kat didn't look back.

Daniel shook his head at Buster. *What was I thinking?* Sure, a casual romance sounded great—in theory. When he'd looked the reality of it in the face, he knew he couldn't do it. Kat was a forever kind of a woman, one who believed in happily ever after—even if she'd never admit it out loud.

And Daniel didn't have forever to offer. Didn't believe it existed without losing part of himself. He couldn't imagine Kat living the life he led in Denver—it would change who she was. And that is what made her the desirable woman she was, quirks and all.

Daniel switched the light off and followed Buster down the hallway. Even the psychotic dog was growing on him. He paused outside the door to his room and watched Buster slip into Kat's room.

Daniel turned away from temptation went into his room and closed the door. He had to keep his mind on his job if he hoped to preserve his hard-earned reputation. Touching Kat again wasn't an option.

Good luck convincing his hands. And his lips. And his body.

It wasn't going to be easy.

Kat listened to Daniel's door close. The sound rang out in the silence of the old house. She hadn't expected him to come to her, but disappointment was bitter, reminding her of the time passing, the years trickling on, and the fear of rejection that imprisoned her in the big bed.

What was she waiting for? A knight to sweep her off her feet? A prince to take her away from everything? Where was it written that a woman had to wait for a man to change her life? She'd damned well be in charge of her own life.

Kat tossed the covers back and sat up. Buster looked at her with watery eyes. ''Stay put, boy. I'm either going to make a fool of myself or I'm going to walk on the wild side. Doesn't matter which, as long as I do something.''

She hesitated at the door. *I can do this. Women do it every day.* Feeling foolish, she slipped into the bathroom and flipped the light on.

Wide eyes stared back at her from the vanity mirror. Kat pinched color into her cheeks. She glanced down at her nightgown. Comfortable, yes. Sexy, no.

She walked to her dresser. Buster rested his head on his front paws and stared at her while she tossed one nightgown after another into a heap. Nothing seemed right for the occasion. What in the world were the dress requirements for seducing a man?

She stepped back into the bathroom.

What did those magazines always say? Oh, yeah. Men are visually stimulated and their emotions don't have to be involved. She didn't want to think about the second part of that at this particular moment. Kat had finally admitted her feelings were affected, but she didn't know about Daniel's.

Kat settled for pulling her robe over a skimpy, thong. She'd tossed the garment into the back of her drawer when Elizabeth had given it to her as a Christmas gift last year. Kat was thankful she hadn't followed her initial inclination and thrown it away. One night might be all she would have with Daniel—she'd make it memorable. Her experience was limited, but she was an imaginative woman. She'd make it up as the night progressed.

Assuming he didn't kick her out of his room on her near naked hind end.

She turned off the bathroom light and drew a shuddering breath. Leaving the front of the robe open, she stepped back into the bedroom and almost fainted.

Daniel waited on the edge of her bed.

Moonlight glistened on his chest and denim covered the lower half of his body. His gaze was fixed on the sliver of skin and thong the open robe revealed.

Kat stared. Why hadn't the dog barked? She looked around for Buster. ''Where's—'' Her throat tightened. ''Where's Buster?''

''He and I came to an agreement. Buster gets to sleep on my bed and in return, he doesn't maul me while I seduce his mistress.'' Daniel patted the bed. ''I hope you're not going to waste my canine negotiating skills.''

Kat hesitated. She'd planned to seduce the man...*this* she wasn't prepared for.

''We can go to the pantry if you'd be more comfortable.''

Slipping the robe from her shoulders, Kat stepped toward the bed and heard bells. All the gibberish she'd read about bells sounding when a person met their soul mate was true. She knew Daniel was the one—now she had proof.

Lifting his head, he stared at her. ''You hear that?''

So he heard them too—he *did* have feelings for her. The bells chimed again, more insistent than before.

''Aren't you going to answer the phone?'' Daniel questioned.

CHAPTER SIX

KAT stared at him. The phone. Of course. Embarrassed, she quickly pulled the robe over her nakedness and walked to the far side of the bed. The phone nearly slipped from her trembling hand.

"Yes?" She wasn't in the mood for polite chitchat.

"It's me," a voice whispered.

Kat glanced at Daniel and raised her shoulders. "Me who? Why are you whispering?"

"I don't want them to hear me, dear."

"Elizabeth?" Kat's voice rose a notch. "Where are you? You don't want who to hear?"

Daniel moved closer and pressed his ear near the phone, trying to listen to the conversation.

''At the phone booth in front of Millie's Drug Store. I saw them. Hurry.''

Daniel made a rolling motion with his hands. Keep her talking he seemed to relay. He hurried from the room.

''Who's them?''

''A couple of shady-looking characters. Didn't like the look of them, so I followed a bit. Strangers in these parts.'' Abruptly, Elizabeth stopped talking.

''Are you still there?''

Kat scrambled about the room with the cordless phone tucked against her shoulder. She was buttoning her jeans when Daniel returned, fully dressed.

''Of course, dear. I didn't say goodbye, did I?''

''No, no you didn't.'' Elizabeth would follow proper social etiquette in a collapsing building. ''We're coming.''

''We, who?''

''Daniel and I.'' Kat pulled her shoes on.

"You don't need to wake him."

"It's okay, he's right here." Kat tied her shoes.

Elizabeth twittered. "About time. Sorry to interrupt."

Kat looked at Daniel and felt the heat rise in her face.

"We'll be right there." She hung up.

"Is she all right?" Daniel looked concerned.

"I think so. I can't imagine what she's talking about."

"Does she do this often?" Daniel followed her from the room.

"Never." Kat chewed her bottom lip.

"We'll take my car. You drive," said Daniel as they left the house.

Kat didn't argue.

Daniel shifted in the seat. There was no comfortable position in his condition. He stared at Kat's profile. *Damn.* He was still aroused from his near encounter with the spunky woman behind the wheel.

Late night phone calls made him nervous. They usually carried bad news. Elizabeth was probably fine, but with everything going on in this case, he wasn't taking any chances.

Kat's knuckles shone white on the steering wheel. He wanted to say something. But, what? ''I liked that thong you were wearing.''

She didn't even look at him. Not a good sign.

''Look, I—''

''Please, I'd rather not talk about it.'' Kat straightened.

Daniel felt something in his gut plummet. ''Regrets already? Nothing happened.''

''Only because the phone rang.'' Her sigh echoed in the car. ''I feel like an idiot.''

Neither attempted to breach the awkward silence again during the three-block drive to meet Elizabeth.

They were nearing the town square. Daniel's gaze darted down side streets and into parked cars. Nothing appeared sinister or out of place.

''There she is, by the phone booth.'' Kat turned the wheel and pulled close to the sidewalk, her brow furrowed with worry.

Daniel was out before the car rolled to a complete stop. ''Elizabeth, are you all right?'' He cupped the woman's elbow and led her to the back door of the car.

Kat had it open, and gave her friend a quick hug. ''Don't scare me like this again. What are you doing out at this time of night?'' She helped ease her into the seat.

''Trying to help Daniel.''

Kat frowned and glared at the man. ''He can handle things on his own. Daniel's a big boy.''

Kat sat in stony silence during the short drive home. *I'm an idiot.* The sight of Daniel's gun had slammed the reality of any relationship they might share into her heart. He was a man with a mission. Only in town to do a job. Then, he'd leave.

Touching him, letting him touch her, had shown how vulnerable she was. It was time to take charge of her hormones and keep her heart from sustaining permanent damage. Only, she had a feeling it was too late.

Daniel kept his eyes on the road, except for glances in the rearview at Elizabeth. Both women stared silently out the windows.

He needed to question the older woman, find out what she'd actually seen—if anything. More than likely it was an overactive imagination. But it still wouldn't hurt to ask.

Kat was another matter—not necessarily easier. She pulled away each time he'd come close to touching her. A far cry from the passionate woman who'd been moving toward him less than an hour ago.

She'd turned hot then cold, but he didn't believe she was a tease. Her desire had seemed as deep as his—she'd wanted the same outcome he'd wanted. So what was wrong? They'd been so close to crossing that line together.

A damned ringing phone, that's what.

For a second, Daniel had actually thought he'd heard bells. The kind that are supposed to ring when you are about to have mind-altering sex. He'd never heard them before. Certainly not with Vivian. He'd do better if he kept those memories in his head, rather than the memory of a half-naked Kat in the moonlight.

Daniel stopped the car in front of the Naked Moon and circled around to Elizabeth's door.

Kat met him before he opened it and whispered. ''I'm going to have her stay here tonight. We can talk to her in the morning.'' She stared over his shoulder, avoiding his gaze.

He wondered if she were using the excuse as a barrier to keep from being alone with him. No, Daniel knew that wasn't it. Kat loved Elizabeth. She wanted to keep her safe.

He opened the door. ''Here we are.'' Daniel offered his hand and helped Elizabeth out.

''Thank you, Daniel. Remember to tell your mother what a good job she did raising you.''

''I won't forget.''

Kat cradled the woman's other elbow. ''I'd like you to stay here tonight.'' She stemmed the expected objection. ''Please, I'll sleep much better.''

Elizabeth looked from Kat to Daniel. ''Very well. We'll talk about the plan in the morning.''

He met Kat's look over the woman's head. Kat raised her eyebrows. Elizabeth seemed determined to be a part of things.

Buster followed them as they directed Elizabeth to Kat's room, trying to redirect some attention his way.

"I'll take Buster for a walk." Daniel whistled and led the way to the back door. "Come on, dog. You owe me." It had been a hell of a night. The dog had slept in his bed, Daniel was sexually frustrated, and Kat was barely speaking to him.

Amazing what a bit of heavy breathing could do for a relationship.

Kat helped Elizabeth into a flannel gown and tucked her in. The elderly woman tried to press for details on what had happened with Daniel. Kat was able to answer honestly. Nothing. Nada. Zilch. Zero.

There *was* no relationship.

She gently closed the bedroom door and went to the kitchen to wait for Daniel.

Tea—that's what she needed. Milk thistle tea to cleanse her body. Maybe it would purge her feelings for the man.

Only one thing could do that. Reverse time and never meet him—it was the only way she'd get him out of her heart. And it wasn't a likely possibility.

Kat went through the motions automatically, missing the joy of the process for the first time in memory. Shoot. The man messed with her karma, disturbed her aura, and warmed her insides. She didn't know which was worse.

The door opened. Daniel and Buster stepped inside with a gust of autumn chill. Daniel crouched on the floor and ruffled the slobbering dog's fur. Buster wrapped his paws about the man's neck and licked Daniel's face.

Jeez—even her "never met a man I didn't want to bite" dog liked the man. With Elizabeth and her dog against her, Kat didn't stand a chance.

Daniel glanced up from his wrestling match. "Mind if I have some tea?"

"I don't mind." Kat brewed an extra cup. "What did you do to Buster?"

His brow wrinkled. "Huh?"

"You're the first man he's taken to." *Just like me.* "I wondered if you were slipping him doggy drugs or something."

Daniel shrugged out of his jacket and tossed the adoring dog a treat. "Nope. I just treat him like one of the boys."

Kat sat at the table. "Don't tell me its some testosterone thing."

"Okay, I won't."

"What you're really saying is that it is?"

He straddled the chair across from her and circled the delicate cup with his hands. "Think about it. The poor guy has lived with a bunch of women. Your great-aunt, you, and Elizabeth."

She nodded. "So?"

"Buster needed a male role model. Guess I'm it."

Kat giggled. The man was unreal. "And how did you figure that out in a couple of days?"

"It's a man thing—you wouldn't understand."

Kat shook her head and watched Daniel pat the adoring dog. Maybe Buster had a sense of the inner Daniel. If her dog thought he was okay, wasn't that enough?

No. Now, not only would she risk her own heart when Daniel left, Buster's was involved and she didn't want her dog hurt.

Kat stopped smiling. "Who are you investigating?"

"I can't tell you that."

"What?" Kat narrowed her eyes. "I'm a part of this."

"I don't involve civilians in my investigations."

"You're not a cop or in the military, so I'm not a civilian to you. Let me get this straight—correct me if I'm wrong." Kat straightened and held a hand up. "You thought I was involved." One finger folded down. "You rented a room under false pretenses." Another finger down. "You searched my room." The third finger disappeared into her palm. No sense mentioning her search. "You're a stranger in town." Four fingers gone. "And, you've turned my dog into a sissy."

Daniel stared at her closed hand. "Don't forget I tried to seduce you."

The heat in his gaze made her squirm. "Yes, well, no need to bring that up."

His gaze darted down to the front of her shirt. She crossed her arms to cover her reaction. The eyes looking at her over his cup told her he knew.

"I want to be involved in this case."

"No."

"I can help. People trust and know me. You're a stranger."

"No."

"I won't stand out like you will. I'll be able to get into places you can't," Kat pressed when he seemed to hesitate.

He shook his head. "No."

Kat slapped the table so hard china and silver rattled. "Daniel West, if you say that word one more time I'll snatch the tongue right out of your mouth."

"Doesn't matter how I say it, the answer is the same."

"It's my business, too. The money I need to save the Naked Moon is missing. Supposedly." Kat leaned forward and gripped his empty hand. "If I can help solve the robberies, I may be able to get an extension until they locate the lost accounts."

"N—"

"I warned you." Kat stood and started around the table. He wasn't going to tell her what she could or couldn't do.

She stood in front of him and tried to intimidate him with a stare. He didn't flinch. ''I'll investigate on my own—Elizabeth will help me.''

''You'll endanger her.''

''Not likely. If someone in this town is crooked enough to be involved with these crimes, I would know.'' Kat lowered her voice. ''Small towns breed familiarity. I can't think of anyone I don't trust in Sugar Gulch.''

''Then you're worse off than I thought.'' Daniel scraped his chair back and stood. He glared down at her. ''It's that outlook that will get the two of you hurt.''

''Just because I trust my neighbors?'' Kat planted her hands on her hips. ''You've been in the big city too long. Things are different here. People are different.''

''There are rotten apples everywhere, Kat. Not all criminals run around with shaved heads and nose rings.'' He leaned closer, putting his nose inches from her own. "I don't want you hurt."

"Oh." Maybe he cared about her.

"I don't want Elizabeth hurt."

"Oh?" The same way he cared about Elizabeth?

"I don't want to lose you."

"Ohhh…" Kat closed the gap between their faces and pressed her mouth to his. He definitely cared about her in a different way than he did her friend.

Daniel pulled back an inch. "If you say that word again I'll have to take the tongue out of your mouth."

Kat wrapped her arms around his neck and pressed her body against his. "Promise?"

His answer was lost as she drew his tongue into her mouth.

Three minutes of bone-melting kisses was all she could stand. Kat stepped out of the ring of his arms. "I can't do this, get involved, and watch you ride out of town.'' She placed the fingertips of one hand against her swollen lips. ''I'm sorry.''

Before the heat in his gaze could lure her back into the circle of his arms, Kat walked away.

She woke hours later to laughter and the smell of bacon. Elizabeth was gone from the far side of the bed. Kat stretched and stared at the canopy. *What am I going to do?*

She drummed her fingers on the bedspread. The last thing she'd waste brain cells on was thinking about Daniel—as a man, anyway. From now on, he was simply the person she needed to crack this case and find her money.

Much easier to say when he wasn't staring at her with lust in his baby blues. Kat smiled. She simply wouldn't look at him. That was it.

Life had been fine before his arrival, it would return to normal as soon as he left.

Normal, but with a gaping emptiness.

Time to let Mr. I-Work-Alone-West know how things were going to run. Kat would be a part of his investigation or she'd start one of her own.

Daniel looked up when Kat strolled into the kitchen. No woman had the right to be that sexy. Her snug jeans and cream fisherman sweater looked as hot on her as her thong.

He shifted. *Have to keep my thoughts away from there.* The thought of another cold shower wasn't appealing.

Elizabeth turned from the stove, spatula in hand. "Good morning, love. My, you look nice."

Kat kissed her cheek. "Thank you. Need any help?" She didn't look at Daniel.

"Heavens, no. Been cooking longer than the two of you put together." She turned to the skillet and flipped thick slices of bacon. ''And I won't forget to save the drippings.''

He rustled the pages of the paper. ''Morning, Kat.''

''Morning.'' She kept her back to him.

Nice as that view was, he wanted to see her face. ''Nice buns.''

She spun to face him, bright spots of color on her cheeks. ''What?''

He pointed at the leftover cinnamon buns on the plate before him. ''I said, nice buns.''

Elizabeth smothered a laugh in her apron. ''Sorry, allergies, they come and go.''

Kat looked in her direction with suspicion, then turned to glare at Daniel.

''Interesting development in the paper this morning.'' He nodded at Elizabeth when she placed a heavily laden plate before him. ''Thank you.''

Kat carried her own plate to the table. ''What's in the paper?''

"Another bank was robbed."

"When?"

"Yesterday evening." He didn't tell her he'd received a call informing him of it after midnight. Global wanted this case solved. Now.

Elizabeth joined them as she slipped Buster some bacon. "Of course it was."

Daniel turned to look at her. "Why do you say that?"

"Well, those nasty-looking men weren't in town for sight-seeing." She took a bite of eggs.

Kat looked at Daniel, willingly, for the first time since she'd entered the room. Her brows drew together and worry tightened her mouth.

He wanted to relieve her anxiety. "What men?"

"Why, the ones I called you about last night." She patted his hand. "Having a senior moment, dear?"

"No, it slipped my mind. Why don't you tell us what you saw and why it seemed strange to you."

"I go to bingo twice a week."

"Yes?"

"Last night, I stayed and talked a bit longer than usual. I'm not usually such a night owl." Elizabeth gave Buster more bacon.

Kat leaned forward. "What did you see?"

"I was walking home, minding my own business. No one can call me a busy-body."

"Of course not." Daniel lifted a brow and glanced in Kat's direction. Elizabeth was the busiest body he knew. "What made you call Kat?"

"When I crossed town square, I realized what a lovely evening I was missing. Did either of you notice the full moon?"

Only while it showed me Kat's body. The blush on Kat's face told him her thoughts had wandered in the same errant direction. ''I noticed—it was unbelievable.''

''So I said to myself, Lizzie Bell—that's what mother always called me—better sit down and enjoy the evening. Winter will be here before you know it.''

Kat touched her hand. ''What did you do?''

''I sat down on a bench next to that old pine. You know the one I mean?''

''Yes, I think so.''

''Wasn't there more than five minutes when I noticed a light shining in the bank window. I could see the shapes of three men, shaking their fists at each other.''

''Could you identify them?'' Daniel hoped he didn't sound too eager. Kat was watching him.

''Not at that distance, but after a couple of minutes two of them stepped out the side door.''

''How did you know they were men?''

''By their size, though I suppose some women could be that tall. But I could hear their voices, not what they said, but they were definitely male voices.''

Daniel bumped his cup, nearly spilling the contents. Maybe she had blundered onto something fishy. ''Did the third person come out?''

''Yes.'' She sipped her tea and seemed to enjoy prolonging the suspense.

''Who was it?'' Kat's voice was edged with exasperation.

''Can't say. The light went out inside and I heard the back entrance door slam, then a car started. It didn't drive by me. That's when I called you.''

Daniel kept his voice even. ''What made you feel the situation was odd?''

''The gun.''

Kat stood, knocking her chair backward. ''What?''

Daniel didn't like where things were headed. How had Elizabeth managed to stumble into trouble?

"In the window. One of the men was waving it about. Not a good idea if you ask me. Not at all."

Kat looked at him with determination in her eyes. "Daniel, may I see you in my room?"

Elizabeth looked up and smiled. "That's the way, Kat. Go after what you want. Don't let life slip around behind you while you're not looking."

Her laugh followed them down the hall. Would he ever understand some of the messages Elizabeth seemed to send Kat?

Kat shut the door after he stepped inside her room and leaned against it. She slowly slid to the floor. "Go ahead and say it."

Daniel leaned a hip against the dresser. "Say what?"

"I told you so." She looked up at him, all color drained from her face. "A gun waved about, in Sugar Gulch. What if something had happened to Elizabeth?"

He crouched in front of her. "Nothing happened. But now, maybe you'll understand I'm not some hormone-packed control freak. I don't want you or Elizabeth hurt."

Kat's eyes widened. "It's him." Her voice was laced with anger.

Daniel kept his emotions off his face. "Him, who?"

"The one you're in town investigating. Chad Filcher." She watched him closely, seeming to wait for him to reveal information.

"Why do you say that?"

She pushed away from the door and paced around the bed. "It all makes sense. Who else would have access to the bank at that time of night? You asked those questions about him." She turned accusing eyes on him. "And you thought I was involved with him."

Daniel shoved his hands into his pockets and kept his mouth shut.

"Don't bother to deny it. You came to the Naked Moon because you thought I was some kind of gangster's girlfriend." Kat walked to where he stood with his fists balled in his pockets and stared him in the eye.

"Not his mistress, but connected somehow." Daniel clamped his lips together. She'd managed to worm her answer from him. What the devil kind of investigator was he?

One who could be distracted by a pair of moist eyes and trembling lips. One who cared too damned much about a woman he had nothing in common with. Except a strong physical lust.

"How could you believe I was involved?"

"You were observed making numerous visits to his office over the past few weeks. I didn't know the reason for those visits until you told me."

Kat rubbed her upper arms and turned to the window. "I suppose I can understand that. But why would he do it?"

"The usual reason—greed, money."

"How much money could he need?"

Daniel resisted the urge to take her in his arms and kiss away the fear he'd seen in her eyes. "Filcher is in deep to some mobsters back east. Gambling."

"Oh." Her shoulders slumped. "You don't suppose Chad knows more about my aunt's money than he's saying?"

"More than likely."

Kat spun to face him. "Then he's been sucking up to me for months, trying to touch me all the time, when he's the one who put me in this position. Risking my business, my home, my inheritance?"

"Oh, I think he's genuinely interested in…getting to know you better." Daniel ground his teeth at the idea of Filcher touching Kat. "Your aunt's money was a convenient way to stay close."

"Then that's how we'll catch him." She narrowed her eyes. "We'll let his disgusting fixation bring him to his knees."

"And how do you expect to do that?"

"By dangling what he wants right in front of his face, making it as tempting and desirable as possible." Kat stared at her reflection in the dresser mirror as if considering how to make herself tempting.

"What are you thinking?"

"It'll take a bit of acting on my part, makeup, a new dress or two, but...yes...I believe we can trap Chad Filcher in his own web."

"N—"

"Don't even think of saying it. You know I'm the best way of finding out what he's up to. I'll get close and get him to confide in me."

"Kat, I won't let you do it."

"It's not a matter of *letting* me do anything. I do it or I confront Chad with the information I have.'' She stared up at him. ''What part of the plan bothers you?''

He turned her until her back pressed against the door, the hardness of his body touching hers.

His face descended. ''The part where he tries to put his hands on you.''

Kat met him halfway.

Mindless minutes passed before she pulled back, breathless, and looked him in the eye. ''Does that mean we trap him my way?''

Daniel covered her mouth with his rather than answer. He hated it, but he knew he was going to let her do it. There wouldn't be a minute he wasn't nearby protecting her.

She was right—Chad Filcher didn't have a chance in hell of resisting what she offered.

Daniel certainly couldn't.

CHAPTER SEVEN

KAT glanced at her reflection in the windows of the bank. She almost didn't recognize herself.

The dress was shorter and tighter than her usual style. Having most of her thighs bared to the world wasn't a comfortable sensation, and the pull of silk across her bust was just shy of obscene.

Several men noticed her walk from the car. Their stares made her feel strange. Sexy, powerful...embarrassed.

The looks some of the wives threw her helped offset it. Kat comforted herself with the knowledge that she'd be able to explain her uncharacteristic behavior once the skunk, Filcher, was behind bars and she had her inheritance.

The bank's security guard opened the door for her.

''Thank you.'' Kat tried to ignore his attention to her legs.

She continued to the secretary's desk and was immediately shown into Chad's office.

Kat strode toward the point of no return and shut the door behind her. She turned to see Chad approaching her with out-stretched arms.

''Kat, what a pleasant surprise.'' He gripped her hands.

She flashed him what she hoped was a brilliant smile. Butterflies tumbled drunkenly over each other in her stomach. She was face-to-face with a possible crook and she needed to play the part of seductress.

Right.

Daniel's face flashed through her mind. He was counting on her, his reputation depended on her. A lot of people needed her to pull this off.

"I hope this isn't a bad time." She resisted pulling away. "I was in town shopping and thought I'd see how the search was going."

He looked her up and down, his gaze lingering on her chest. "Is that a new dress?"

"It is—how kind of you to notice." Kat pulled her hands free and executed a spin. Kat struck a pose. "You don't think it's a bit much? It's not my normal thing, but I was in the mood for something different."

"Oh...no...it's..." Chad ran a finger under his collar, pulling it away from his pasty neck, "...charming. Makes the most of your...coloring."

She crossed to the chair in front of his desk. Sitting, she demurely tugged down on the skirt. It stretched to cover another quarter inch of her skin.

"I'm afraid it's shorter than it appeared on the mannequin." She begged silent forgiveness from Mrs. Conrad who'd raised her eyebrows when Kat asked her to hem it to such an ungodly short length.

Kat looked up through her lashes to see Chad's gaze fastened on her thigh. He licked his thin lips.

She needed to distract him before he pounced. ''Is there any word on my aunt's money?''

Chad walked behind his desk and sat in the chair. He rolled it closer to Kat, but he couldn't reach her hand across the wide expanse of wood.

''I wish I had good news for you, but I'm afraid nothing has come up…uh,'' he glanced at his lap and shifted in his chair, ''since the last time we met. I'm sorry.''

Kat ran her tongue over her lips and gave him her best wide-eyed pout. ''How much time do I have before the bank will take action?''

''Two, three weeks at the most.''

She put her arms on top of the desk and mashed her breasts together to enhance her cleavage. *Forgive me, feminists of the world.* ''I'm not sure what to do, Chad. I'd hoped to find a way out of this on my own...but time is getting tight.''

Chad didn't answer, his stare focused on the cleavage displayed. A shiver of revulsion ran across her shoulders.

His eyes nearly bulged out of their sockets.

He actually thinks I want him. Gag me with thick, black coffee.

The intercom buzzed. Twice. Chad pulled his gaze from her chest and pressed the button. ''Ye—'' His voice broke. ''Yes?''

''Your one o'clock appointment is here.''

''Just a moment, please.'' He turned back to Kat. ''I'm sorry, if there was any way to cancel this appointment, I would.''

She stood and smoothed the dress with her hands. ''I understand. You're an important man.'' She turned toward the door.

"Kat?" He moved to stand directly behind her.

She faced him warily. "Yes?"

"I'd like to take you to dinner, maybe
over to Bakersville." His gaze never left
her breasts.

"Are you sure that would be appropri-
ate?"

"What do you mean?"

"My being a customer of the bank..."

"Nonsense, I see whomever I like." He
sidled closer. "And I want to see you."
His oily smile made her skin crawl.

"I'd like to have dinner with you." Kat
batted her eyelashes. "Will eight be too
late? We may end up being out most of
the night?"

"I'll pick you up." He moved closer.

Putrid pimples. Chad was going to try
to kiss her. It would be the supreme test
of her mettle as an actress. *I have to think
of Daniel and the Naked Moon.*

He leaned toward her cheek. Kat gritted her teeth and turned her head at the last second. His mouth landed square on hers.

Chad was too shocked to take advantage before she stepped back and lowered her eyes. ''Until tonight.''

Kat didn't notice anyone in the crowded bank in her single-minded effort to put as much space between herself and Chad as humanly possible.

Another planet would be nice.

Daniel didn't like it. The minute Kat stormed into the house she'd rushed into her bathroom and locked the door. The shower had been running for twenty minutes.

He pounded on the door. Again. ''Kat, are you okay?''

Silence was the answer to the question he'd asked her three thousand times in the past twenty minutes. If that scum had hurt her, Daniel would kill him with his bare hands.

The shower stopped.

Daniel perched on the edge of the over-size bed and waited. She'd have to come out eventually.

The door slammed against the bathroom wall when Kat yanked it open. Muttering to herself, she pulled drawers open and whipped garments out. She obviously didn't notice him.

But Daniel noticed her. The towel wrapped and tucked above her breasts was generous but not too generous. The long length of leg it revealed raised his blood pressure. On top of the last twenty minutes of worry, it wasn't a good thing.

''What the hell happened with Filcher?''

Kat jumped. The panties and bra she'd chosen slipped from her fingers. ''For the love of—you nearly gave me a stroke.''

Glancing at her attire, she looked up at him. "Don't you dare look at me like that!"

"Like what?"

"Like...like a man." She scooped her clothing off the floor.

"Can't help it—I *am* a man."

"Then stop it." Kat stomped to the bathroom door.

"Did he hurt you?" Daniel strode toward her, determined to get an answer.

"Only if you count wanting to scrub every inch of my skin with lye soap." Kat crossed her arms over her chest. "I've never felt so...so...violated in my life. That dress is a slime magnet."

"I warned you—how did you expect the man to react?" Daniel touched her shoulder, the skin soft and damp beneath his fingers. Big mistake. He yanked his hand back. "Did he rise..."

Kat blushed.

''Sorry. I mean did he fall for the line?'' The clean smell of her tugged at him.

''Hook and all.'' She backed into the bathroom. ''I don't think he looked me in the eye for more than ten seconds, total.''

''And?'' Though it was difficult, Daniel concentrated on looking her in the eyes.

''And I'm having dinner with him to-night. A late dinner.''

''I don't like it. I should be the one do-ing this.''

''Hardly. The dress wouldn't have had the same effect if you'd worn it. Face it, I'm in this until we nail him.'' She pushed the door halfway closed. ''You're doing it again.''

''Doing what?''

''Looking at me like *that*.'' With that, Kat shut the door.

What had she expected? He knew what temptations the towel hid. One small tug on the corner of the towel and it would have been...heaven.

Huh. More likely a black eye.

Kat wandered into the kitchen. The worn jeans and comfortable sweatshirt soothed her. Helped her to put the blue dress out of her head for a while.

Elizabeth stood at the sink, peeling carrots, and humming. Kat stood next to her and laid a gentle hand on her shoulder. "You don't have to do this."

"I know, dear. But it makes me feel useful. You and Daniel need time together."

"We don't need time. I told you, there's nothing between us."

Elizabeth tut-tutted. "Goodness, you're protesting a bit much. I was referring to the case. The one you're helping him with."

She felt herself flush. "I knew that. Has Daniel filled you in?"

"Oh my, yes. He's quite conscientious about his work." She glanced warningly at Kat. "I don't like you having to get close to Chad. Never liked him."

Kat picked up a paring knife and attacked the first carrot she grabbed. "I can handle Filcher. But, if I find out he had anything to do with Aunt Bernice's money turning up missing, he'd better hope I don't have access to any sharp objects."

The mound of carrots quickly dwindled. Kat simply pictured each one attached to Chad and treated it appropriately—peeled it, chopped it in half and cut it into strips.

"Why don't you lie down for a while? Otherwise, I won't feel right about you helping with high tea."

Elizabeth smiled at her. "Seems I recall saying the same thing to you about twenty years ago."

"You did, didn't you? I'd forgotten."

Elizabeth gave her a quick hug. "You never forget, dear. It's always in your heart.'' She shuffled out of the kitchen leaving a feeling of peace in her wake.

Smiling to herself, Kat placed the carrot sticks in a bowl of water. She glanced around the kitchen for Buster—the poor boy needed her attention. The last few days had been bizarre and she'd neglected him. Where was he?

She whistled. ''Buster, come here, boy.'' Nothing.

If he were in the house she'd have heard the clicking of his nails on the hardwood floors. Kat grabbed a baseball cap and jacket from the closet and stepped outside. Robust laughter drew her to the side yard.

Man and dog rolled on the ground, tangled in each other, covered with golden aspen leaves. They were too caught up in their game to notice her.

Kat leaned against the house and enjoyed the view. Each took turns topping the other. Buster's tail wagged so vigorously, she feared it might knock Daniel out if it made contact with his head.

Daniel's laughing eyes looked up and locked with hers. Neither looked away. Kat felt the pull. The wanting…the desire. Why this man? Why now? She wanted to roll on the ground, toss leaves in the air, and have Daniel lay over her. She wanted it all.

Buster launched himself onto Daniel's back and broke the sensual interval. It was just as well—nothing could come of it.

Daniel stood and tried to brush some of the leaves off his clothes then walked toward her. Buster trotted obediently behind him.

"What have you done to my dog?"

"Nothing." Daniel looked down and scratched the dog's ears.

"Nothing? You've turned him into a first-rate wuss." Kat reached up and plucked a leaf from Daniel's hair. Her hand froze when she saw the heat in his gaze.

"He's not totally ruined—I taught him a new trick."

"Okay, I'll bite. What new trick?" Anything to avoid his knowing gaze.

Daniel walked to the pile of leaves and stuck his hand in, shuffling it about for several seconds. "Aha." He removed a neon green round disc. "Just keep your eye on this aerodynamic plastic disc."

"It's a Frisbee."

"Shh. Buster likes it to sound complicated." He bent his wrist and widened his stance.

The Frisbee flew into the air, lifted by the breeze. Buster tore after it. Twisting his body at an unbelievable angle, he grabbed it in midair. Obviously gloating, he ran to Daniel and dropped it at his feet.

Kat clapped. "Good boy." Daniel looked at her with a smug smile. "I meant the dog."

Daniel knelt and gave Buster a belly rub. The besotted dog whined in ecstasy. Kat could understand. She'd experienced the ministrations of those long fingers, imagined them stroking her skin again, stoking a fire within her.

Stop. Think of Chad Filcher. Think of rabid bats. Anything but remembering how good Daniel's body felt, how hot his mouth had been. It was no good. She wanted to feel the heat again, get close enough to get singed.

''Aren't you hot?''

Kat blinked. ''Hot? What?''

Daniel smiled at her. He seemed to know the effect he had on her. ''With your jacket on, I mean. It's warm out here.''

''Only if you've been rolling around with a hyper mutt.'' She shivered. ''Normal people feel chilly this time of year.''

''Normal? Normal?'' He tossed a handful of bright leaves her direction. ''Honey, normal is not a word I'd use to describe you."

Honey. He called me honey. I like it.

"Oh, and you think being a stuffed shirt like you is normal? Never believing in anything unless a government agency approves it? Sneaking around people's homes at night? Touching women's panties?"

He grinned wickedly.

"In dresser drawers." Kat picked up the Frisbee and launched it. Buster didn't move.

Daniel looked down. "Go get it, boy." The dog took off like a fly after butter.

Even her dog responded for the man. Kat turned to go inside. Man and dog deserved each other.

But what was she going to do with her brokenhearted dog when Daniel left? How was she going to help Buster get over the man? How would she get over him?

*   *   *

Seven forty-five. Daniel checked his watch again.

Elizabeth patted his arm. "Now, you're working yourself into a frenzy. Our Kat will be fine, she knows how to take care of herself."

Seven forty-six. He felt a moment's panic. Only a few minutes left before bank-scum picked Kat up for their date. The kitchen shrank with each second ticking away.

"I can't let her do this."

"I think you know that Kat makes her own decisions. You may as well accept it. Makes a relationship easier."

"We don't have a relationship." His voice didn't ring with conviction. Was wanting a relationship the same as actually having one? Not likely. "What's taking her so long?"

Kat answered from the doorway. "A woman wants to look her best when she crushes a bug.'' She stepped into the kitchen.

The sound of her heels on the floor was assured. Her exotic perfume reached out and seemed to grab him. Daniel swallowed. The hot pink, v-necked sweater was two sizes too small. And her breasts...her breasts were all but spilling over the top and the snug black skirt stopped well above her knees.

Daniel folded his arms across his chest. ''No way.'' Possessiveness took over his brain functions.

Daniel glared at her. Seven forty-eight. ''Go change.''

''No.''

Elizabeth cleared her throat. They both turned to look at her. ''You'll be following her, right, Daniel?''

''Yeah, but—''

''No buts. She needs to keep Chad distracted while she gets information out of him.'' The elderly woman pushed her glasses onto the bridge of her nose and peered at Kat. ''That outfit should more than do the job.''

Daniel and Kat glared at each other. He wanted to drag her back to the bedroom and rip the bra off her. Plus her sweater, skirt, panties—hell, he just wanted her naked. The thought of the banker groping her all night made him want to pound something.

The doorbell rang.

Eight o'clock.

Kat wobbled on her heels, her angry color replaced by pallor.

Daniel pushed his personal feelings aside to reassure her. ''I'll be right behind you or nearby in the restaurant. If you can't see me at any time, get away from Filcher. And get back here.'' He turned to Elizabeth. ''You'll stay by the phone in case she calls. I'll have my pager on vibrate. Buster will stay with you and we'll lock the doors behind us.''

Clicking her heels together, Elizabeth gave a jaunty salute. ''Yes, sir.''

''You're a cheeky girl.'' Daniel grinned, thankful for the tension breaker.

''Don't you forget it, snapper-head.''

The doorbell's buzz was insistent.

Kat's gaze was wide and panicked. ''I can't do this, Daniel. What if I can't see you? What if he tries to touch me?'' She put a hand on her stomach. ''I'm going to be sick.''

Daniel pushed her toward the front of the house. If they stopped this charade now, Filcher's alarms might go off. As much as he hated it, Kat had a chance at getting the information. ''You're going to be great. Filcher's jaw will drag the ground and you'll have him eating out of your hand.''

She smiled. ''Thanks. Now step out of sight.'' Kat opened the door after he slipped into the darkened parlor.

"Chad, I'm sorry to keep you waiting." Her voice was low, seductive.

Chad was enjoying his eyeful. Daniel watched through the small slit in the door and wanted to leap out and pummel the man. *What the devil's wrong with me?* This was the reaction we wanted from the outfit. Unfortunately.

"That's all right." Chad tugged on his tie. "You look...wow."

"Thank you. I hoped you'd like it." Kat handed her cape to him.

Chad slipped it over her shoulders, practically drooling into her cleavage. Daniel clenched his fists.

"Where are we going?" Kat asked.

Grasping her elbow, he turned her to the front door. "The Brass Bear. I've heard spectacular things about their chef."

"That's in Bakersville?" She enunciated each syllable.

Too aroused to notice anything odd, Chad nodded. When they stepped outside and closed the front door, Daniel and Elizabeth moved out of hiding.

Elizabeth glanced at him out of the corner of her eye. "They make a handsome couple."

"Trying to make me jealous?" Daniel glared at her and slipped the jacket of his suit on. He hated suits.

She wasn't intimidated. "Heavens, no, dear. You're already way past there without my help. Now, get going and follow my girl."

He did.

Kat grimaced in the darkness of the car. She glanced backward. Still no headlights. Where was Daniel? Why did the drive to Bakersville have to be so isolated?

"Warm enough?" Chad continued with his inane chatter.

"Yes, I'm fine." Ah. Headlights glimmered behind them in the distance. Reassured that Daniel was nearby, she focused her attention back on Chad. "Tell me what it's like to be in charge of so many people at the bank and so much money."

His chest swelled with self-importance. "Why trouble your pretty head with boring business? Let's talk about more interesting things—like you."

"You probably know everything about me."

"I like to listen to your voice," he encouraged.

Did women actually fall for his lines?

"I've been running the tearoom since I was fifteen, except for the time I spent in college, and Aunt Bernice left it to me when she died." She gave a sniff for effect.

Chad reached his unoccupied hand out to comfort her. It landed on her thigh.

Like my leg needs comforting.

"Anyway, things were going well until the mortgage note came due. That's when

I discovered the money was misplaced at the bank.'' She covered his wandering fingers with her hand before they crept higher. ''I'm tired of worrying about money.''

''I'm sorry. We're doing everything we can to locate it.''

''And I can't tell you enough how much I appreciate your help.''

Chad's hand crept higher. ''I'll find a way to remove this worry from your life. You and I have a lot more in common than I think you realize.'' He glanced sideways at her chest.

''We do?''

''I've noticed your adventurous spirit. You want to see the world, the big cities, tropical paradises. Sugar Gulch is a backwater town to you, too.''

''Why...how did you know that?'' Kat hated the simpering in her voice.

''It's in your eyes. You deserve more than waiting on people and dishing out that brown water you brew.''

Kat bit her lower lip until she tasted blood. If he said one more condescending word about her tea, she was going to claw his eyes out. Case or no case. The thought cheered her.

The man's ego knew no bounds. Hadn't any woman ever said ''no'' to him, turned away his pathetic advances? No, apparently he was a rejection virgin. Kat couldn't wait to be the first to burst the bubble of his arousal.

Kat slid to the center of the bench seat. ''Deserving more and getting more are two different things.''

His foot slipped off the accelerator but he replaced it immediately. ''You couldn't be more right. It's the people who are willing to take a chance—grab what they want—that get it.''

Kat closed her eyes and pictured the one time she'd grabbed what she wanted. Daniel. The pantry. Her lips parted as she remembered the heat of his touch.

Parched, she moistened her lips with her tongue. She opened her eyes and glanced into the rearview mirror. The recipient of her grab in the dark still followed.

Stay close, Daniel.

Their arrival at the Brass Bear saved her from more useless prattle.

The restaurant was posh, elegant and re-fined. Kat hated it on sight. Snooty people eating snooty food, looking down their noses at anything edible not pronounced with a French accent. The maître d' led them to a secluded corner. Dim lights and candlelight added to the atmosphere of privacy.

Kat slid to the back of the booth hoping to avoid physical contact with Chad. No such luck, he slid next to her until the length of his thigh pressed against hers. Her appetite disappeared.

''Wine?'' Chad whispered in her ear.

Maybe she could liquor him up and get information easier. ''Please.''

"A bottle of Talbot Monterey Chardonnay." Chad closed the menu and continued speaking to the waiter. "I'd like the Roasted Duck with Autumn Vegetables. And the lady will have the Braised Sirloin Tips with New Potatoes." The waiter discreetly vanished and Chad turned to her.

"I hope you don't mind my ordering for you. I'm hopelessly old-fashioned."

You don't think I have a brain, you twit. "Oh, no. I probably would have mispronounced something." Kat barely kept the sarcasm from her voice.

A server approached with their wine and offered Chad the cork. After an arrogant sniff and then a taste, he nodded and the waiter poured two glasses.

Chad lifted his glass in a toast. "To the most beautiful and tempting woman in the room."

Their glasses touched and Chad drank. Kat touched her lips to the alcohol and pretended to enjoy it. After his second glass of wine, dinner arrived. Kat glanced around the room looking for Daniel. Finally, she spotted him several tables away, behind an enormous fern.

Kat distracted Chad with conversation and made sure the waiter refilled his glass when it emptied. Chad didn't notice that hers never needed refilling, probably because his focus was on her breasts.

"So...tell me what I can do to make all...your dreams come true." Chad's breath nearly knocked her off the seat.

She leaned closer. "Help me find some easy money."

The clatter of crashing dishes made her jump. Kat looked up to see that Daniel had knocked over a waiter in an attempt to jump out of his booth. *Great, I almost had Chad talking.* She needed to divert her date's attention—fast.

Grabbing his thigh, she whispered in his ear. "Maybe we could take the long way back to town."

He was hers—not that she wanted him. Chad motioned for the check.

In less than three minutes they stood outside, waiting for the valet to bring the car. Chad swayed in the breeze, and tried to nibble on the back of her neck.

''Here's the car. Would you mind if I drove?'' She couldn't let him behind the wheel in his condition.

Chad shrugged and leered at her. ''Anything you want.''

When she slid behind the wheel, it was to find Chad in the middle, all but on her lap. Kat put the car in gear.

Two minutes later, Kat regretted her decision to drive. Chad had two hands free to grope her. It seemed like twelve.

She pushed his hand from under her skirt and tried to remember why she was in this situation. ''You were telling me how you were going to make my dreams come true.''

"Lots of money, babe." He nuzzled her ear with a slobbery mouth.

"You mean you've saved a lot of money?"

"Ha—" Hiccup. "That's the sucker's way. Need to have bigger dreams."

Kat felt an hour-long shower with bleach coming on. No amount of information was worth this. Searching the road behind her, she didn't see headlights.

Come on, Daniel.

A glance at Chad showed him barely able to hold his head upright. If she could delay a couple more minutes he'd be out for the night. But she needed him to talk. She needed to buy time for Daniel to find them. Kat yanked the wheel and stomped the brake. Tires screeching, she pulled onto the shoulder.

Chad blinked. "What's going on here?"

Kat unbuckled her belt and turned sideways. "I want you. Right here. Right now.'' She knew time was against her in his condition. How could she have known he was a lightweight drinker?

''Course you do.'' Chad raised one hand but it fell uselessly to his side. ''Come closer, like a good girl.''

Questions she could try later—she just wanted the nightmare to end. Kat slid closer, turning her face to avoid his rancid breath. Chad's face landed in her cleavage.

One sloppy kiss on the swell of her breast and he was snoring.

Now what?

The crunch of gravel sounded behind the car. Daniel.

Kat twisted her neck and glanced back. He strode to the car with fists clenched.

''Get the hell off her, Filcher.'' He grabbed the door handle.

''No. Daniel, don't—''

He yanked the door open and Kat felt herself falling backward. Daniel caught her and stopped her descent. Chad slid down, too. His face now rested comfortably in her crotch.

"Get him off me." Kat tried to push the dead weight away.

Daniel blinked. "What happened?" He pulled her from beneath the snoring man.

Steadying herself against the car, she glared at her rescuer. "What happened was you weren't there. Behind me. I had to improvise. Thank God he passed out before I had to get rough."

"You're the one who dragged lover boy out of the restaurant at the speed of light. It takes a while to pay the check, you know." Daniel stepped closer. "You scared the hell out of me."

Kat glowed inside. He'd worried about her. "Yeah, well, here we are." She jerked her head toward Chad. "And there he is."

"I'll follow—you drive him. We'll go back to his house and put him on the couch.'' He pushed Chad to the far side of the seat.

''Okay, but if he grabs me in his sleep, I'm pushing him out of the car.''

Twenty minutes later, they stared at the man sprawled across the leather couch. He hadn't even opened his eyes when they'd half dragged, half carried him inside.

Kat shook the hair out of her eyes. ''Now, what?'' She kept her voice low.

''Give me your panties.'' Daniel held his hand out.

''What?''

''We'll leave them on the floor, next to the couch. Bank boy will think he hit the jackpot and your relationship will be on a whole new level.''

Kat clenched her teeth. ''Turn around.'' After he turned, she peeled her panties off.

Thank heaven for thigh high stockings.

''Done.'' She tossed them on the floor, heat rising on her neck.

Daniel glanced down at the garment she'd discarded. "No thong?"

"For him?" She nodded at Chad. "Not on your life."

"Good. Let's go."

Good. Kat mulled that one word all the way to the car.

Daniel held her door then ran around to start the car. Seconds later, they were headed across town. He parked in front of the house and killed the engine.

She reached for the door handle.

"Wait." His voice low and husky. "I'm sorry for losing you back there for a while."

"It's all right. It turned out okay."

"But it might not have. Filcher could have—"

Kat pressed her fingers against his lips to stop his words. "He didn't." She tried to lower her hand, but couldn't. Daniel's lips opened slightly and he licked her fingers.

It was a light touch, but it raced though her like pure electricity.

''Daniel, we shouldn't.''

He kissed her palm. ''Why not?''

Why not?

''Because you'll be leaving.'' All of her inner fears of losing her heart to this man resurged.

''I'm not going anywhere right now.'' Daniel moved his hot mouth to her wrist.

Her pulse beat wildly against his lips. Kat squeezed her eyes shut, then opened them. ''Someone could see us.''

Daniel looked around at the lights in neighboring houses. ''I'll meet you.''

She felt breathless and daring. ''Where?''

''Our place.''

''Oh.''

''The pantry.''

CHAPTER EIGHT

AN HOUR later, after seeing to Elizabeth and Buster, Kat finally stepped into her room and slipped out of her shoes. She should be exhausted, but a heightened sense of desire had her wired.

Can I do this? Of course she could. She wanted Daniel more than she'd ever wanted any man in her life. And he obviously wanted her. But was it enough? She didn't have his heart and probably never would.

Kat tossed the sex kitten outfit in the corner and stepped under the shower's spray. Scented gel helped erase the memory of Chad's hands on her skin.

She lingered, fantasizing about what could happen in a pantry the size of hers. Anything and everything. She turned the

206

shower off. Enough was enough, Kat wanted reality, not fantasy.

The tile floor was cool beneath her feet, but she dried briskly and hurried to her room. Again, the dilemma of what to wear. Sultry and obvious, or sensuous and sweet?

She rubbed a touch of jasmine oil on her pulse points. Never hurt to take advantage of a natural aphrodisiac.

Kat looked at her pale face in the mirror. No more delays. What was it that raunchy disc jockey on the radio always said? Oh, yeah. Put up or shut up.

She wasn't in the mood to shut up.

Daniel wanted Kat so much it was becoming painfully obvious. He couldn't believe he was about to have a late night encounter in a pantry. Not the usual run-of-the-mill location for a seduction, but then, Kat wasn't an ordinary woman.

Each minute he spent with her pulled him in deeper.

Daniel watched the play of light from neighboring houses. Each its own little world filled with families. People who cared about each other. People who took pains not to hurt the ones they loved.

What if Kat ended up hurt when he left Sugar Gulch? This was becoming too complicated.

When did I start to feel something for this woman? And, what the hell am I going to do about it?

He dropped to the edge of the bed.

Nothing. Not a damned thing. He couldn't risk hurting Kat—the pantry wasn't a good idea. Daniel turned the lamp off and lay back on the spread. Sleep would be a long time coming.

Kat held her breath and reached for the knob. She hesitated. All she had to do was open her bedroom door and walk down the hall. Easy.

She wanted more, needed the whole cup of sugar, words of love and devotion. In fact, Kat wanted Daniel in her life forever, not just a night or two.

Her arm dropped to her side. She turned and slipped between the sheets of her lonely bed and stared at the wall. A lone tear found its way down her cheek and dropped off onto her gown.

She rubbed her cheek with the back of her knuckles. Maybe he wouldn't mind being in the pantry by himself. There were plenty of cinnamon rolls left over. Kat knew he liked her buns.

The ringing phone woke Kat. She fumbled for the receiver, and knocked the clock onto the floor. Six-thirty. Who was calling this early? The phone stopped ringing.

Kat pulled a pillow over her head and tried to doze off. Someone pounded on her door.

"Go away." Kat rolled toward the opposite wall.

The door opened. She looked over her shoulder to see Daniel and Elizabeth framed in the doorway. Daniel held the cordless phone out to Kat but she barely noticed.

His chest was bare and the top button of his jeans was still unfastened. *Oh, Lord.* The man was a walking advertisement for temptation. Daniel cupped his hand over the mouthpiece. "It's lover boy."

Wide awake, Kat struggled upright, holding a sheet across her chest. "Give it to me."

Daniel stepped closer to give her the phone and he and his elderly accomplice settled onto the end of her bed. They picked up the extension and leaned their heads together to listen.

"Good morning."

Chad cleared his throat. "Kat, my dear. Can you forgive me for my behavior last night? The wine—"

"Don't think another thought about it. It was delicious wine—I overindulged myself." Kat rolled her eyes.

"And to think that even after my deplorable actions you...we..."

She made gagging motions. "Well, things did get a bit out of hand, but I have no complaints."

"Were you...I mean did I..." Chad paused. "Could you get pregnant?"

Kat shook her head at the thought of the man ever reproducing. Daniel and Elizabeth waited to hear her answer. "I hadn't thought about that. You drove that idea out of my head last night."

"When can I see you again?"

Kat hesitated and looked into Daniel's eyes.

Chad rambled on. "I'd like to have a clearer memory the next time."

In your dreams, pal. "I'd like that, too."

Daniel shook his head, his meaning unmistakable. She ignored him.

"How about lunch?" Chad begged.

"I think I can make that. I don't have a lunchtime tea scheduled today." She stuck her tongue out at Daniel. Elizabeth smiled indulgently.

"And, Kat?"

"Yes?"

"Let's make it a long lunch." He hung up the phone, ending the nauseating conversation.

Elizabeth giggled.

Daniel stood and towered over Kat. "Didn't you see me shake my head?"

"Yes." She angled her chin upward daring him to push her further. One idiot man at a time was all she could handle.

He glared at her. "You are the most stubborn, infuriating female I've ever met."

Kat smiled. "Thank you. Now if you'll take yourself to another part of the house,

Elizabeth can help me pick an outfit to please my lunch date.''

He sneered. ''Save yourself some time and toss a coat on over that thong thing.'' Pictures rattled when he slammed the door on his way out.

Elizabeth wagged a finger at her. ''Now, dear, he's just concerned for your safety.''

''I know. It's just that he rubs me the wrong way.''

''More likely, he rubs you the right way and that scares you.''

Kat slipped off the edge of the bed. ''I'm not scared.''

''Prove it. To yourself.'' Elizabeth stood in front of her and held her hands. ''Don't let something special slip through your hands because you don't know what will happen tomorrow. That's half the fun of living.''

She gave a push toward the bathroom. ''Now get in there and get to work. You have a snake to step on.''

*   *   *

Daniel dialed the number from memory. It was answered on the third ring.

"Global Insurance, Bob Reynolds speaking."

"Bob, Dan West. You must be busy." Daniel leaned against the icebox.

"Why don't you get your scrawny butt back here and find out?" Papers rustled in the background.

"All in good time. Any news on that background I requested on Filcher? Everything I have is full of holes." He glanced toward the hallway.

Slurping sounds came through the phone. "Arrived thirty minutes ago."

"I'll need it faxed, but are there any high points I should know about today?"

Pages turned. Bob muttered. Daniel pictured him scanning with one hand and holding his life-sustaining coffee in the other.

"Here we go—no steady girl, but he's a ladies' man wannabe. Business degree, appointed bank president three years ago.'' Bob laughed. ''One brush with the law, back during his sophomore year of college. Someone reported a dead body in his dorm room. Turned out to be one of those blow-up bimbo dolls. Bet he had a rough time living that down.''

''No doubt.''

Daniel heard voices in the hall. ''I need to hang up. Thanks for the help.''

He was reading the paper when the women walked into the kitchen. Flipping the page, he noticed Kat's outfit and his groin tightened instantly.

''What do you think?'' Kat spun. ''Elizabeth chose it. Said it was guaranteed to bring a man to his knees.''

Or his back, on top, or any way she wanted it. Daniel stared, trying to form a coherent thought in his mind. Unfortunately, the blood from his brain had settled elsewhere when she'd strutted into the room. No, he had to be honest—

Kat didn't strut. She had no clue what she did to a man.

"It's—" His vocal chords entered their second puberty. "Nice."

"Nice?" Kat walked up to him and pulled the paper he hid behind from his hands. "Look again, mister. This is the latest in naughty."

Oh, it was. The knit sweater dress fitted like a second skin, only closer. Every dip and curve was accented and it stopped mid-thigh. Daniel looked into her eyes. Hers widened in response. No wonder— his lust had to be all but tattooed across his face.

Her expression turned wary and she walked away. "Never mind."

The sway of her hips hypnotized him. He glanced at Elizabeth and she flashed a thumbs-up his way.

What was that for? In this house, who knew? He stalked to his room to regroup.

An hour later, he was in the kitchen coaching Kat on undercover technique. ''Try to get him to brag, confide, whatever. But don't endanger yourself to do it.''

She wiped her palms on the dress. ''It feels strange, having Chad assume he and I...you know.''

''Hopefully, it will work to our advantage.'' Daniel offered her a small recorder. ''I wasn't sure the caliber of crook we were dealing with last night, but I think you'll be okay with this. Keep it in your purse. Try to flip it on if he starts blabbing about the banks.''

''Okay.'' Her voice sounded small and unsure. ''You'll be close by?''

''Right outside the bank. I'll follow wherever he takes you for lunch.''

Elizabeth rose and crossed her arms purposefully. ''I'm going with you.''

''I don't think—'' Daniel and Kat spoke at the same time.

"You take me or I follow on my own. I'm a part of this—I picked the outfit. Never know when a senior citizen will come in handy on a, what do you call that thing? Oh, stakeout."

He didn't trust her not to follow through with her threat. It would be better to keep her where he could watch her. "All right, but you do exactly as I say."

Elizabeth smiled triumphantly. "Yes, dear."

Daniel watched Kat turn the "closed" sign in the front window. "Will you lose much business?"

She shrugged. "I figure if I don't find my inheritance money, I'll lose a lot more."

Everyone was silent. She had a good point.

Buster whined from the backseat of Daniel's car. How he'd been roped into the dog coming along, he had no idea. But when Kat and Elizabeth decided something it was best to step out of the way. When had his investigation turned into a circus? How was he supposed to keep them safe?

Kat opened the passenger door. ''I'll try to steer Chad someplace within walking distance.''

Daniel grabbed her hand before she stood. ''Be careful. The man has more arms than a roomful of chairs.''

''Like you have to tell me. I smacked every one of them last night.'' She turned to Elizabeth. ''Be gentle with Daniel—he's not sure what to make of you and I yet.''

Daniel watched several male heads turn to watch as she walked into the bank. He wanted to strangle the life out of each and every one of them. No, that wasn't true. He just wanted Kat. And that scared him more than facing down a crowd of felons.

He turned to his backseat guest. "Now we wait. The exciting part of a stakeout you never see on television."

Elizabeth pulled her knitting from a bag and settled back. Smart woman. He could use something to divert his thoughts from what might happen in Chad Filcher's office.

Kat tried to keep the desk between the banker and herself. She'd hiked mountain trails that took less energy.

Kat rolled the chair between them. "Wouldn't you like to get some lunch?"

"Darling, everything I'd like to sink my teeth into is already here." He caught her about the waist. "Let's refresh my memory about last night."

Kat squirmed in his arms. "I'm a little hurt that you don't remember."

"In ten minutes you'll be wishing you hadn't left last night." Chad fastened his mouth on her neck.

The intercom buzzed. Chad jammed his finger on the button. ''I don't wish to be disturbed.''

''I'm sorry, Mr. Filcher. You insisted I let you know when Mr. Granger called. He's holding on line two.''

''Thank you.'' Chad straightened and the color drained from his face.

Interesting.

Time to make it impossible for him to ask her to leave. She slipped her hand inside his jacket and rubbed his chest. He looked from her to the phone and back. Decision time. To make sure he chose correctly, she slipped a button of his pristine white shirt through its hole.

Grinning, Chad plopped in his chair and pulled her onto his lap. One of his cold hands rubbed her thigh while the other reached for the phone. ''I'll only be a minute, then you can unbutton anything you like.''

She smiled into his beady eyes. *I'd like to button your lip and sew your fly shut.*

"Mr. Granger, sorry to keep you waiting. Inefficient staff," Chad lied.

Kat took a deep breath and nuzzled his neck. The phone was only an inch from her ear.

"You're out of time, Filcher."

Chad's hand stopped. "But I gave you the information you asked for two days ago."

"So you did." Granger paused. "We've decided one more code and delivery date will wipe your slate clean."

"One more?" Chad swallowed and glanced toward Kat.

She pretended to be oblivious to the conversation.

"Which one?"

"Yours."

Chad sat upright and Kat nearly tumbled onto the floor. He grimaced an apology and pulled her against him. "When?"

"Now. Tonight." The answer brooked no opposition.

Chad appeared to collapse within himself. "You'll have it."

The connection was severed and he dropped the phone onto his desk.

Kat traced the outline of his mouth with a fingertip. "Everything all right?"

His attention focused out the window. "Everything hasn't been all right for a long time."

Her voice lowered suggestively. "Can I help take your mind off it?"

Chad smiled sickly. "Not even your many…gifts…could do that." He lifted her from his lap. "I hate to ask, but I'll need a rain check on lunch."

Kat suppressed a relieved smile. "And I was so looking forward to dessert."

His eyes brightened. She hurried to the door before he could change his mind and waggled her fingers at him. "Call me."

The wind rushed past her as she hurried from the office, far from Chad's groping hands.

She plowed into someone coming in the front door. ''I'm so sorry.''

Strong fingers encircled her upper arms. Startled, she looked up. Daniel. ''What are you—''

He pulled her into the bright sunshine. ''Getting you out of there. What happened?'' They hurried toward the car. His arm wrapped around her waist.

Daniel's support felt good and helped erase the memory of Filcher's touch. ''Getting close to the suspect. Isn't that my job?'' She couldn't keep the snap from her voice.

He yanked the door open. ''Are you okay?''

Buster licked her face and Elizabeth put a hand on her shoulder. Surrounded by people who cared, Kat smiled. ''Yeah, I'm okay. Let's go home so I can fill you in on the latest developments.''

Daniel's gaze bored into hers for long seconds before he shut the door.

The drive home was quiet. Kat simply wanted time to reflect on what she'd learned.

After Daniel parked the car in front of the house, Kat walked Elizabeth home. The older woman wanted details, but Kat insisted she rest. ''There will be plenty of time to talk this afternoon.''

Daniel wasn't so easily appeased. He followed two steps behind her through the house.

Kat stopped in front of her room. ''The details can wait until I change.''

''Five minutes.'' He stalked to the kitchen.

Kat flung the latest garment of lust into the back of her closet. At the rate she was going, it would be necessary to burn her entire wardrobe.

Four and a half minutes later she strolled into the kitchen. In her jeans and T-shirt with her face scrubbed clean, she felt almost human.

Daniel concentrated on pouring the hot water into two waiting teacups. Kat's snug shirt made the job feel like rocket science. He glanced down at Buster who watched him with rapt adoration on his muzzle. *Why can't Kat look at me like that?* Without the slobber, of course.

''Any special tea blend?'' she asked.

''The jar was labeled wild raspberry. I'm not sure what it's supposed to do.'' Daniel concentrated on steeping the leaves as if it were brain surgery, anything to take his mind off the jeans molding her legs.

''I like it.'' Kat smiled and pulled a chair out. ''Need any help before I sit?''

''Believe it or not, I think I've gotten the hang of this.'' He shook his head. ''If the guys could see me...''

"What?"

"Well, brewing tea is not an everyday thing for me. I hadn't even tasted the stuff until you poured it down me." He carried the cups to the table and settled into a chair. "Okay, enough chitchat. What happened?"

She inhaled the tangy aroma wafting up in the steam. "He's in it up to his eyeballs."

"Great! You recorded him?"

Kat stirred her tea and avoided his gaze.

"Tell me you have it on tape," he begged.

"I couldn't. It was a phone conversation. I'm sorry."

Daniel swiped his hand down his face. "It's not your fault. How did you hear a phone conversation?"

"You don't want to know." Kat sipped her tea to hide her face and nearly boiled her tongue. "Ouch!"

''That's what you deserve. Answer my question.''

She lifted her chin. He was *not* going to make her ashamed. ''I sat on his lap while he talked on the phone.''

He dropped his spoon, a look of horror on his face. *''What?''*

''Well, I could tell by his face I needed to hear the call. That was the only way to keep my ear near the receiver.''

''And, where were his hands while you sucked on his neck?'' Daniel glared at her.

She leaned back in her chair. *Maybe he's jealous? Dream on, tea girl.* ''Stop acting like Father Confessor. You sent me in there to get information. I did it. End of story.''

''But, you—''

''Did something I detested. If it brings him down, it will be worth it. Aren't you interested in the phone call?''

''Damned straight I am. Did you get a name?''

"Granger. Chad nearly had a stroke when his secretary buzzed the call through."

His fist slapped the open palm of his empty hand. "That's the connection."

"Come again?"

"The mobsters Filcher owes. Granger is high in the organization."

"How high?"

"The FBI would love to get their hands on evidence against him that would stick." Daniel leaned forward. "What did he say?"

"They mentioned information Chad had passed to him. Asked for more. Something about codes and delivery dates."

He stared into his cup for several minutes. "That would explain a lot."

Kat grew impatient. "Like what?"

"Why the banks were hit soon after a big cash delivery. How the thieves know which days to hit once the bank is closed.'' He drummed his fingers on the table. ''If Filcher is passing the security codes to their computer systems and delivery dates for each branch, it explains a lot of coincidences. As bank president he'd have access to that information.''

She felt the blood drain from her face. ''If that's the case, we have a problem.''

''What's new?''

''I think the Sugar Gulch bank will be hit next.''

Daniel straightened. ''Did Granger say that?''

''Not in precise words—he demanded the codes and dates for Chad's bank. I think it's safe to make that assumption.''

''Without proof, we can't pull anyone in on it.''

''I *heard* it,'' she said.

''Doesn't hold up in a court of law.''

''Where does that leave us?''

Elizabeth walked into the room. ''Why can't someone confront him? Tell him the game's over.''

Kat shook her head and smiled. ''I thought you wanted to rest.''

''No, dear. *You* thought I needed a nap. I thought I needed to keep up with what's going on.'' She placed her oversize purse on the counter. ''So, what do you say? We barge into his office and get the worm to confess?''

''No—the law is filled with loopholes. A lawyer would have him out in less than an hour.''

''Then play Filcher and Granger against each other, see what happens,'' Kat suggested.

''Possible, but we need concrete outcomes, based on fact, that will hold up during a trial.''

Elizabeth stood behind Kat, a hand on her shoulder. ''Can't Kat wear one of those bug things?''

Daniel smiled. ''You mean a wire. Too risky—he might find it.''

Kat was outraged. "He would not! Just how far do you think I'm willing to go to convict the man?"

"Settle down, dear. Daniel's just worried about you. No telling what Chad might do if cornered."

Kat and Daniel faced off across the table. Tension pulsed in the air. Neither backed down.

Elizabeth looked from one to the other. "That's enough quibbling." She gently chided, "You almost made me forget what I needed. I have to go to quilting at church for the afternoon. But I need some boxes moved up from my basement. I hoped you could do it while I'm gone."

Daniel broke eye contact with Kat and looked at the woman. "Just tell me which ones."

She turned toward the door. "There's no time. I'm late already. Kat, would you be a dear and point out those charity boxes you helped me pack?"

Kat smiled, determined to ignore Daniel. ''Of course. When are they coming to pick them up?''

''In the morning. You can stack them on the sunporch.'' She patted Daniel's cheek as she passed. ''It's so nice to have a strong man around.'' The door banged behind her.

Kat glanced at Daniel from under her lashes. He did look strong. She shook her head. No thinking of him as a sexy man— a passionate man. He wouldn't sneak past her defenses again.

He stood. ''Let's take care of it now before you start on your night tea stuff.''

''High tea.'' Kat led the way out of the house and into the one next door.

''Whatever.''

Oh, this should be fun.

Daniel stared down the dark steps into Elizabeth's basement. ''Where's the switch?''

Kat flipped it. The bare bulb at the bottom cast shadows. "It's not much—these old houses added electricity long after they were built."

"Let's do this without breaking any bones. I'd hate to use sick days because I tripped down a flight of stairs." Daniel stomped into the basement.

He was acting as tense as she felt. It wasn't like she was the one acting macho and bossy.

Kat glared at his back all the way down. They stopped at the bottom and looked around. The packed dirt of the tiny space emitted a dank, earthy smell. "That stack against the far wall."

"Fine. I'll take it from here."

"Oh, please. Do I have useless dame stamped on my forehead? I'll help." If he treated her like a dense child again she might flick the back of his ear.

"Can't you listen once, instead of jumping in?"

Kat's shoulder's stiffened. ''All right, out with it.''

''With what?''

''You've treated me like a pariah since we left the bank.''

Daniel turned away and lifted a box. His broad shoulders made the small area feel smaller. ''It's your imagination. Don't get hormonal on me.''

She blocked his path. ''Why is it when a man doesn't want to talk he screams *hormones?*''

''Because it's one of those squirrely girl things.''

''You, sexist, ignorant, pigheaded—''

''Ah, ah, ah. Watch your language. There are spiders present.'' Daniel smiled.

Kat saw red. For the first time in her life, she understood the overused cliché. Frustrated, she gave the box he held a shove.

Daniel stumbled back a step, hovered and almost regained his balance until he stepped on a discarded shoe. Tripping, he fell back and lay still under the box.

Oh, no. She'd done it again—injured the man. Kat knelt next to him and yanked the pile of spilled clothing from his face.

He stared at her. ''Almost a full day.''

She rocked back on her heels. ''What?''

''I went almost a full day without you inflicting a bodily injury on me. The percentages are going up. Seems to be a habit.'' The box tumbled to the floor when he sat up.

A door slammed. Kat jumped. ''Criminy, you're bad luck.'' She walked to the bottom of the stairs. ''I'll wait upstairs while you play he-man.''

Daniel grunted and she hurried up the stairs. She reached out and turned the knob. Nothing happened. Kat pushed. Nothing. She wiggled the doorknob. It turned.

Oh, please. Anything but that. Had the broom been near the door? She'd forgotten to check.

The sound of Daniel scraping clothes off the floor carried in the quiet. She tried to swallow past the wad of cotton that seemed to have taken up residence in her mouth.

Her shoulders sagged. *This isn't happening.* She slipped back down the stairs. ''Daniel.''

He ignored her.

''Daniel,'' she spoke louder.

He sighed. ''Now, what?''

''The door.''

''Yeah?''

She motioned toward the panel of wood. ''It's stuck.''

CHAPTER NINE

KAT waited for the explosion.

"For the love of...I'll take care of it."
Daniel jogged up the stairs and pushed on
the door. "It's not locked—the knob
turns."

"I know."

"Okay, Kat, I give up. Why won't the
door open?"

She hesitated.

"Kat?"

"A broom usually leans on the wall
next to the door."

"So?"

She cleared her throat. "I think it fell
and slammed the door shut."

He drummed his fingers on the door.
"And?"

"It might have...could have...wedged behind the refrigerator."

"Are you speaking from experience?"

She sighed. "Yes. It happened when I was about twelve. Scared me half to death. Luckily Elizabeth was in the house and heard me yelling."

Daniel descended the stairs. "Kat?"

"What?"

"How long will Elizabeth stay at quilting?" His voice was deceptively calm. She could hear the tension straining to explode.

"Two hours, more if she stays to chat with the pastor's wife." She backed up a step. "This isn't my fault."

He stopped six inches away and stared down at her. "No? Name one rotten thing that's happened to me since I arrived in town and tell me you weren't involved."

She couldn't. "That's not fair. How do I know you weren't accident-prone before I met you?"

"You are the most maddening, frustrating, impulsive—"

Kat felt her bottom lip quiver. She bit it to keep it still.

"Don't you dare cry and make me feel like the bad guy."

She poked his chest. "I don't cry. Ever. Especially over something a know-it-all, pushy man says." To her horror, she burst into tears. Not roll-down-the-face-quietly tears. But noisy, raspy, messy, snotty tears.

Daniel looked trapped. His hands came up to hover over her shoulders. "Aw, Kat, stop it. I didn't mean to bark at you."

His words only made it harder to stop. "This is it! First I hit you, then I stand you up in the pantry, I have to let old fish lips Filcher paw me, and now—"

"What did you say?"

She quieted herself. "I said, fish lips—" Loud sniffles echoed in the tiny space.

''No, about the pantry.'' Daniel rested his hands on her shoulders.

''Just that I'm sorry I…that you waited…that I didn't go to the pantry to meet you.'' She stared at her feet.

''Kat, look at me.''

She shook her head. If he accused her of acting like a child, so be it.

He put a finger under her chin and forced her to meet his gaze. ''I didn't go to the pantry either.''

''You stood me up?'' She pushed his hand away. ''How dare you. How did you know I didn't stand there in my altogether and wait for hours?''

His fingers clenched her shoulders. ''Did you?''

''Did I what?''

A heat burned deep in his eyes. ''Think about coming to the kitchen in the altogether?''

She stared at his lips. ''What do you think?''

He groaned. ''We have to get out of here.'' Daniel scanned the walls desperately. ''Is there a phone?''

''No.'' She watched him pace the floor.

''What about Buster? If we yelled, he could find someone and lead—''

''He's not Lassie, and the way he was snoring, there's no way he'd hear us.''

Daniel stopped. ''We're stuck then.'' He looked at the stack of boxes. ''Are they all full of clothes?''

''I think so.''

''Dump them.''

''What?''

''Do you see anything resembling a chair? A pile of clothes will be a lot more comfortable than a dirt floor.'' He opened a box and turned it over. ''Why couldn't this be a big, bright, modern basement?''

''Because, this isn't a big, bright, modern house. Thank goodness. It has character.'' She helped him dump the boxes, then surveyed the mess. ''Elizabeth is going to kill us.''

''Not if we die of starvation before she finds us.'' His growling stomach punctuated his words.

''For heaven's sake. Do you always panic in unusual situations?'' Kat walked to a nearby shelf and removed a glass jar from the dozens that were stacked. She held it closer to the light. ''Peach jelly, fresh this summer.''

The lid twisted off with a pop. She stuck her finger in and scooped some out with her finger then offered the jar to Daniel.

He ignored the jar and wrapped his fingers around her wrist. She stared at him, mesmerized by the intensity in his eyes. Oh, my.

Now she understood his need to escape. The pull between them made use of their circumstances, led them toward something they'd tried to fight.

Daniel pulled her peach-drenched finger to his lips. His tongue darted out and tasted the fruit, then licked the rest from her flesh. ''Who needs a spoon?'' The husky words melted her, turned her insides to molten mush. He dipped his finger into the jar she held and waited.

Kat looked at the finger and the sweetness coating it. She leaned forward and took it into her mouth. Closing her lips, she stripped the goodness from his skin.

Daniel closed his eyes and moaned. ''I've tried to leave you alone, Kat. I swear.'' He smeared jelly on her lower lip.

''Who asked you to?'' She held her breath, waiting.

He didn't disappoint her. He licked every drop from the fullness.

''What are we afraid of?'' Kat used two fingers and smeared his throat. ''I want to live—taste everything.'' Her tongue fulfilled the promise of her words. No stickiness remained on his skin after she licked it clean.

Daniel dropped to his knees in the soft pile and pulled her down with him. Only inches separated them, their breathing bordered on panting.

''I don't want to leave you with regrets.'' His face was shadowed in the faint light.

She placed the jar on the ground and reached for the bottom edge of his shirt. ''If I don't touch you, I'll regret it for the rest of my life.'' She lifted upward and pulled the shirt over his head. Golden hair covered his muscled chest, tempted her to touch and explore.

Daniel watched her with hooded eyes. She gathered her courage and scooped more jelly. His eyes slid shut as she smeared it down his chest to the place where the trail of hair disappeared into his jeans.

Carefully, so as not miss a single drop, Kat cleaned her mess. Daniel's chest heaved with each breath he took, the heartbeat under her mouth wild and uncontrolled. It matched hers.

She raised her face and kissed his chin. ''Hungry?'' Her voice came out low and husky. She was amazed to still have the power of speech with the force of the desire coursing through her.

A low, feral, growl was her answer. Daniel yanked her shirt over her head before she could think to be shy. She felt heat rise in her face as he stared at her demi-cup, push-up bra. Her heavy breathing all but tumbled her breasts over the top.

He picked up the half-empty jar. ''Dessert before supper.'' A glob dropped onto the swell of her breast and slid into the shadowed cleavage. Daniel's greedy gaze followed the path it left on her skin.

She waited. He smiled, teasing her. Kat decided to let him know what she wanted, in case it wasn't clear.

''Daniel, I—''

Footsteps sounded above them. Time to return to real life. Whatever that was.

Elizabeth had smiled when she'd released them from the basement with a knowing look in her twinkling eyes. They'd explained about the lack of chairs and offered to fold the clothes.

It was a good thing Elizabeth moved slowly or she would have had an eyeful.

Daniel followed Kat to her house. He watched the sway of her hips and felt his jeans tighten. Not even ten minutes had passed and he wanted her to taste her lips again. They'd enjoyed each other, nothing had happened that both hadn't wanted.

The phone was ringing when they stepped inside.

Kat hurried to answer it. "Hello." She grimaced. "Chad, I'm glad you called."

Daniel clenched his hands into fists, wanting to pound Filcher's head against pavement. It wasn't jealousy he assured himself. Kat was her own woman, helping him with a case. But the thought of another man touching her drove him insane.

Not waiting to hear more, he stalked to his room. A cold shower would take his mind off of Kat's hot, wet body and the soft sounds she'd made in the back of her throat as they touched each other.

Daniel slammed his bedroom door and marched, stiff-legged, to the shower, clothing trailing behind him on the floor. He had to stop thinking about Kat or he'd do himself bodily injury.

The ice-cold spray pelted him in the face.

Kat finished a quick shower and dressed. Chad's phone call worried her, and so did

Daniel vanishing into his room before she'd finished.

Brushing the tangles from her hair, she relived the frantic moments in the basement. Waves of heat washed over her and her breasts swelled beneath her thin shirt. The brush slipped from her nerveless fingers and she gripped the edge of the dresser with both hands.

Facing her reflection in the mirror, she faced her unspoken fear—the possibility that the interlude might be all she had of Daniel.

At least she had that, the tenderness of her swollen lips was a reminder. Her heart would carry the only reminders she'd have once he left, but she didn't regret one delicious minute of it.

A knock yanked her from her tantalizing musings. She faced the door. ''Yes?''

Daniel stepped inside. ''We need to talk.'' He glanced toward her massive bed. ''Can you meet me in the kitchen?''

Coward. ''I'll just be a minute.''

The door closed behind him.

How could he be so unaffected when her body hummed from the terse interaction? Darn, she had it bad.

Moments later she faced an angry Daniel across the linoleum covered floor of the kitchen.

''From here on out I handle the investigation.'' He crossed his arms over his chest. ''It was wrong of me to involve you at all.''

Kat planted her hands on her hips. ''I don't remember you asking. I make my own decisions.'' Who did he think he was? ''Believe it or not, I managed to run things just fine before your head met my skillet. What makes you think you can order me out now?''

''This isn't a game.'' Daniel paced back and forth. ''Granger takes this to a higher level of risk. I won't have you involved.''

He faced her and ran a hand through his hair, a frown marring his face.

"Bite me." Kat's voice was deceptively calm. Anyone who'd known her for any length of time knew what the tone forewarned. She was going to blow.

"Excuse me?"

"I. Said. Bite me." Kat enunciated each word to ensure he understood. "Translated, it means, take a flying leap, butt out, or who do you think you are?" She crossed her arms. "Take your pick."

A cheerful voice chirped behind them. "I'd take the flying leap." Elizabeth stepped into the hostile arena with Buster on her heels. "You two neglected this poor baby, so he came scratching at my door."

Kat and Daniel stared at each other for several tense seconds before Daniel turned away and crouched to rub Buster's ears.

The older woman looked from one to the other before speaking. "What are you two fussing about? Here I thought the pile of clothing on my basement floor boded well for your relationship.''

Kat frowned. ''We don't have a relationship.'' She avoided Daniel's eyes. ''Mr. Testosterone told me to stay away from his investigation.''

''So?''

Kat sputtered. ''My money is involved, too. My efforts with Chad, disgusting as they were, dredged up good information.''

Daniel stood and defended himself. ''Efforts? You all but danced naked on the man's desk.''

''How dare you!'' Kat poked his chest. ''I distracted him to get what you wanted.''

''I certainly didn't want him to fondle you.''

''He didn't, not exactly.''

''If we continue, he will.'' He stared into her eyes with concern.

Kat's anger deflated in the face of his genuine emotion. "Would you care?"

Instead of answering, Daniel turned to Elizabeth. "I'm taking the poor neglected dog for a walk. Will you try to talk sense into her?"

Kat muttered under her breath when he left the house. "Arrogant nincompoop."

"You have it bad." It wasn't a question.

"No I don't. He's uptight, a control freak, bossy—" Kat broke off to glare at her friend. "What are you smiling about?"

"Oh, my dear, listen to yourself." She laid a gentle hand on Kat's arm. "If you truly didn't care, he wouldn't have you so furious."

Kat shook her head. "I don't want to have it bad. I don't want to care."

"Why ever not? He's a fine man."

The tears came, fast and stinging. "Because he'll leave. And I don't want to end

up hurt.'' She let Elizabeth wrap concerned arms about her and cuddle her as
though she was ten years old with a
scraped knee…instead of a twenty-eight-
year-old with a breaking heart.

Daniel followed a curious Buster down the
street. Scents and sounds distracted the
dog and he investigated and returned.

*That's what I need—the attention span
of a dog.*

Maybe then he could remove the memory of Kat's angry and accusatory words.
She had a right to be mad, but it didn't
change the way he felt. He wanted her out
of the case, as far from Filcher and
Granger as possible.

He tossed a stick for Buster. *Who am I
kidding?* The thought of Filcher touching
any part of Kat made him crazy. Kat was
too trusting. She could get in over her
head without realizing it. If something

happened to her... Daniel kicked at a rock. What would he do?

The minx had wriggled her way into his heart. He just hadn't wanted to see it or admit it. No attachments, that was the way he liked his relationships with women. And he always admitted that up front. He dated women looking for fun and companionship, not family.

Kat was different. She'd given parts of herself to him without asking for promises in return.

So what was eating him? That was the way he wanted it...wasn't it?

Buster frolicked with a couple of kids in a leaf-strewn yard. The children laughed as the dog licked their chins, dashing from one to the other, giving his affection freely.

Daniel stopped as though someone had slammed a lead ball into his midsection. He wanted it all. Kat's love, his babies growing in her belly, and the idiot dog whining to be let out in the middle of the night. When had it happened? He'd only known the woman for a matter of days. And most of those had been spent arguing or recovering from injuries she'd inflicted.

How had love entered the picture? And what if she didn't feel the same way? He frowned, remembering. She hadn't uttered one word of her feelings.

Hands shoved deep into his jacket pockets, Daniel continued walking. A smile crept over his features. That's it. Kat thought he'd blow out of town as soon as the case was solved, leaving her behind. Miss Smear-Condiments-and-Forget-'em had another thing coming. His step grew lighter thinking about proving to Kat he wasn't the love-'em-and-leave-'em type.

A visit to the local law enforcement office sounded like a good idea. The best idea he'd come up with in a lifetime.

Buster ran to keep up with him.

*   *   *

Elizabeth frowned.

Kat tried again. ''Please. I didn't have a chance to tell Daniel about the phone call. If I don't do something now, his investigation could be shot.''

Her friend remained unconvinced.

''Look, Chad wants to see me tonight. But he said it would have to wait until after his meeting.'' She grasped Elizabeth's hands. ''What other meeting would he have at the bank after hours? He's going to pass the information. Without pictures or a recording, what kind of proof will Daniel have?''

''Daniel said it could be hazardous.''

''It doesn't have to be. I'll keep my distance, stay out of sight.'' Judging by Elizabeth's expression, Kat was gaining ground. ''I'll just snap a couple of pictures of the exchange, maybe record their voices and, bam, we'll have the proof. Daniel keeps his reputation and I keep the Naked Moon.''

Elizabeth nodded. "Your motivations are pure. I'll go along with it on one condition."

Exhilaration raced through her veins. "Anything."

"I go with you."

Kat's shoulders sagged. "You know you can't. If something happened—"

"I make my own decisions."

Kat's words came back to haunt her. "This is different."

"Is it?" Elizabeth stood and grabbed her purse. "I'll grab my camera and meet you at your car."

Kat's mind scrambled for a way to keep Elizabeth safe.

"Don't even think about abandoning me. I'd have to find Daniel and send him after you." Elizabeth scolded.

Kat shook her head ruefully. The woman was just pigheaded enough to do it.

That's probably why we get along so well.

CHAPTER TEN

DANIEL wiped sweat from his forehead with his shirtsleeve and squinted up at the late afternoon sky. Two hours of intense questioning and strategy wore a man down.

The fall chill swept across his damp skin, sending chills up his spine. He looked around. Where was the dog? Daniel really hadn't expected to find the brute. Hell, he wouldn't have stood out in the wind for two hours.

Kat was probably spoiling Buster right now, rubbing his belly and talking about how rotten Daniel was to abandon the poor baby. He zipped his jacket and jogged toward home.

Home. The word tumbled about inside his head. When had the Naked Moon become home? That was easy—the minute his heart realized where it belonged. Too bad it had taken his fool mind longer to figure it out.

Daniel rearranged his priorities in his mind. He had a job ahead of him. Not the bank robberies, that was child's play. No, this job was more important.

Daniel had to convince Kat to trust him with her heart, to believe that total opposites could be attracted. His future, his life, depended on it. And his heart.

Daniel's eager steps slowed and finally stopped. Dark. All of the windows in the house were dark. He glanced at his watch, its luminescent dial showing the time. High tea should have been in full swing. Instead, a closed sign showed in the front window.

He automatically slipped his hand under his jacket to check his weapon. The restraining snap released under his well-practiced fingers and Daniel crept around the side yard.

What the hell was going on? A glance to the right showed dark windows at Elizabeth's.

Get a grip. They probably went shopping together.

His gut knew differently. Years of listening to his instincts told him this wasn't normal. He wasn't going to stop listening now. The crunch of footsteps on leaves sounded behind the house.

Daniel eased forward and peered around the corner.

Seconds later, a massive shape barreled into him and knocked him on his back. Annoyance replaced shock when the dimwit dog licked his face.

''Get off me you overgrown gerbil.'' Daniel shoved the animal with both hands. Buster tucked his tail between his legs and whimpered.

Daniel felt two inches tall. It wasn't the dog's fault he liked him.

Daniel stood and scratched Buster's head. "Sorry, boy, but you scared me out of twenty years of life. Plus you bruised my ego getting the jump on me." He looked around. "Where's your mistress, hmm?"

Buster tilted his head and grinned. As much as Daniel had ever seen him grin. Loping off, the dog stopped at the back door and waited for Daniel.

"All right, let's find out what's going on." Daniel opened the unlocked door and slipped inside.

Darkness and silence greeted him. Buster ran ahead and looked in each room, then returned and stared at Daniel.

I don't like this.

The hairs on the back of Daniel's neck bristled. Filcher was involved—he could feel it. So, should he call the sheriff and tell him he had a "feeling" something wasn't right? Sure. And he'd be in a holding cell for observation while Kat and Elizabeth were unaccounted for.

A blinking light caught his eye—the answering machine. Daniel punched the button and listened, impatiently, while it rewound.

''Kat.'' Filcher's voice spoke from the box. ''The meeting I told you about has been moved up. I'll be able to pick you up earlier than I thought.'' The voice lowered. ''I'd like to see you in that tight sweater number.'' Click.

Daniel ground his teeth. It didn't take a rocket scientist to figure out where the women had gone. Now, if they were only okay, he hoped he could restrain himself from putting Kat over his knee and spanking her backside.

Infernal, headstrong, reckless woman. What in the world had possessed her to go after Filcher on her own?

*   *   *

Kat rubbed her chilled arms. *What am I doing here?* She glanced at her car parked across the park—Elizabeth's head was visible through the window in the faint glow of streetlights.

She should be home enjoying a cup of tea. The cold wasn't comfortable on Elizabeth's joints. Turning her collar up, she stared into the window of Chad's office.

It was a quarter after seven and he was still alone. Where was this big, bad mobster? Perhaps they'd been wrong—Chad wasn't involved. Right. And Daniel spent the afternoon buying her an engagement ring.

Kat knew Chad was involved up to his beady little eyeballs—she just had to prove it. She wasn't going to let the weasel ruin Daniel's reputation. Or that other thing, what was it? Oh, yeah, the money for the tearoom. How could she have forgotten?

The chill numbed her bottom. That's it. Standing, she brushed the crumbled leaves from her jeans.

Kat gave what she hoped was a reassuring wave to Elizabeth and strode to the bank's side door. Patting her coat pockets, she checked to be certain the camera and recorder were still in place.

She pounded on the door, then smoothed her hair. Time to become the sultry seductress. Chad's pinched face appeared when the door swung open.

''What are you doing here?'' His eyes darted left and right before he grabbed her hand and jerked her inside. The door slammed behind her, loud and final.

''I thought you wanted to see me tonight.'' Kat ran a fingertip down the front of his rumpled shirt.

''Yes, of course, but I left a message. Told you I'd come by your house.''

''I'm sorry, I haven't been home to check my machine. Can you forgive me?''

Chad's features were indistinct in the feeble light, but the lust in his eyes was blatant. He wanted her and he'd take her against the wall if she'd let him. Kat resisted the reflex to gag. She needed to lure him to the office, where Elizabeth could see them.

It wasn't much, but it made her feel safer.

''I was hoping you'd show me your office again.'' She unbuttoned the top button of her shirt. ''That great big, solid desk.'' Another button sacrificed itself for the greater good.

Chad's tongue darted over his thin lips. ''Yes, oh, yes. But we'll have to hurry. I'm expecting...a client.'' He took her elbow and led her past empty cubicles until they reached his office.

Kat led the way inside. ''Hurry? I was hoping we could take it slow this time.'' She rested her hip against the desk, making sure to keep Chad faced away from the window. "Our last date was rather awkward and rushed. I want to take the timetoappreciateyourtalentstonight."

Chad's inverted chest swelled with pride as her well-directed flattery stroked his ego. "Oh, Kat, I guarantee you'll be screaming my name in unbridled ecstasy."

She beckoned him closer with a crook of her finger. He opened the front of his white shirt.

All thoughts of his expected guest were obviously forgotten.

Chad reached her and fastened his fish lips on her neck.

Kat moaned with revulsion. Chad took it as a sign of arousal and circled kisses around her neck. Kat glanced toward the window and froze.

No. Daniel stared at her, fire blazing in his furious blue eyes, witness to her humiliation.

Frantically, she waved him away with her hand behind Chad's back. He was walking into the situation blind. He didn't know about Granger being expected.

Chad lowered his attention to the swell of her breasts. Kat laced her fingers in his hair to pull him away. When she looked up, Daniel was gone.

''Why, Kat, I never took you for the rough type.'' Chad growled.

Kat placed her hands on his chest and pushed. Chad fell over his own feet and landed on his butt. She reached into her pocket and activated the recorder.

Shock etched his features, replaced by anger. ''Rough is one thing, Kat, but a man likes to call the shots in matters of intimacy.'' He struggled upright while she buttoned her shirt. ''I decide when and how I'll have you.''

''I don't think so.'' She had to distract him, give Daniel a chance to protect himself. "Game's over. It doesn't go any further."

Chad yanked his shirt closed. "Like hell. You don't let a man go this far and not follow through."

Kat backed around the desk. Where was Daniel? Where was Granger? She needed to push some buttons. "I know everything."

Chad paled but didn't back down. "What do you think you know, Kat?" He continued toward her.

"The bank robberies...my aunt's money."

Still he advanced, not looking as unassuming as before. "You don't know anything."

"Granger." The one word stopped him like a brick wall.

Anger became fury in his eyes. "And here I thought you were such a smart girl. It's not very smart of you to come here by yourself.'' He buttoned his shirt. ''You used me. That's hard on a man's ego.''

Kat glanced toward the window hoping for a glimpse of Daniel and Chad grabbed her arm. She tried to wrench free, but he held her in a viselike grip.

''People know I'm here,'' she warned. ''They'll be looking for me.''

''Please, if others knew about me, you wouldn't be here touting your ample wares.'' Chad pressed her against the wall while he reached into the bottom desk drawer. The gun he pulled out was small, but authentic. He pressed it against her side.

Fear raced through her. Kat searched her mind for anything to distract him. ''Why'd you take my aunt's money?''

''Personal reasons.'' Chad pressed himself suggestively against her hip. ''It was a way to stay close to you, get into your bed. Only you were a tougher nut to crack than I'd planned.''

He yanked her toward the door. She had to give Daniel more time. "So it's not tied to the robberies?" Where was Elizabeth? Kat prayed she was still safely in the car.

Chad chuckled. "My darling girl. Your money is peanuts compared to what I'll get from this bank."

"But I thought Granger—"

"Not bloody likely—this time *I* reap the benefits. He'll be blamed, of course." Chad flipped the lights off.

"You'd double-cross a mobster?" Daniel's voice echoed in the near darkness of the bank.

Thank goodness. She backtracked. No, not good. Daniel still didn't know about Granger.

Chad pulled her in front of him. "Who's...who's there?"

Her captor trembled like a dollar bill in a windstorm. "Daniel, no he's—"

"Shut up, you stupid girl," Chad squeaked in her ear. "Daniel, who? The writer? Damn—I should have guessed it was too coincidental.''

''Filcher. Step outside so we can talk.''

''I...don't...'' He cleared his throat. ''I don't think so. You see, I have Miss Bennett. And I have a gun.''

Silence. Kat strained her eyes trying to locate Daniel. Chad moved them closer to the door.

A shadow darted past the window. Chad pointed and pulled the trigger. Nothing. He pulled again. Nothing. It wasn't loaded.

Kat stomped on his foot and shoved her elbow into his chin.

He jerked backward and released her arm.

I'll remember to thank Daniel for letting me practice that move. Kat dropped to her knees and scrambled behind a nearby desk. She heard Chad scampering in the opposite direction.

Running footsteps headed toward the back of the bank. A thud sounded and chairs clattered to the floor. The sound of fists on flesh reverberated in the darkness.

Daniel. What if he was injured? *No one hits him but me.*

Kat charged into the darkness.

CHAPTER ELEVEN

DANIEL grabbed Filcher's shirt and shoved him against a desk. The dog had touched Kat. Threatened his woman.

He landed another blow on the man's mouth.

A hellcat leaped onto his back and knocked him sideways. Filcher scrambled away.

''So help me, Chad, if you touch him again I'll remove your manhood with a dull spoon.'' Kat pummeled his back with her clenched fists.

Daniel reached back and yanked her over his shoulder and onto the floor, then pinned her arms above her head. ''Kat, I swear if you hit me again, I'll spank you.'' He felt her stiffen beneath him, then relax.

Her hands slipped free of his loose grip and snaked around his neck. ''Daniel, I'm sorry, I thought Chad was—''

''Shh...he's still in here.'' He yanked her to her knees and shoved her toward the closest desk. ''Crawl under there and stay put or so help me, I'll—''

Kat slipped beneath the desk.

''That's better.'' Daniel moved toward the back of the bank. Where's Filcher? Silence answered him. He felt along the wall and found a doorway beneath his hand.

''It's the men's room.''

He twisted and pressed Kat against the wall. ''I told you to stay put,'' he whispered in her ear.

She touched his cheek. ''I was worried.''

He relented. She'd been through hell tonight. ''Stay behind me—can you do that?''

''Yes.''

Daniel braced himself, kicked the door wide and charged in. Bright lights blinded him.

"Oops." Kat stood with her hand on the switch.

Filcher burst from a stall and knocked him backward. Daniel watched his gun skitter across the floor. He grabbed the banker and rolled him onto the floor.

Kat stared. She flipped the lights off, then on again.

"Get...the...gun." Daniel landed another blow.

Kat rushed to the gun and scooped it into her hands. The barrel wavered and light bounced off the chrome.

With my luck, she'll shoot me. Daniel focused on the banker.

Filcher clipped his jaw. The gun steadied in Kat's hand.

"Hold it right there," she barked.

Both men froze—Chad out of fear and Daniel out of worry that she'd accidentally shoot *him.* He moved and cuffed the banker to the urinal, then slipped beside Kat to pry the gun from her fingers and hold it on the man who'd dared to touch her.

''You did good, Kat.'' Daniel smiled and watched her slip to the floor.

His fearless Kat had fainted.

Kat moved her head. The pounding was excruciating. She eased her eyes open. *Where am I?*

Everything came rushing back and she sat upright. Dizziness swept over her. She was in the backseat of a police car.

Elizabeth patted her hand. ''Now, now, dear. You're safe.''

Kat scanned the crowd outside the window. ''Where's Daniel? He's not safe.'' She pulled her hand free. ''I have to warn him about Granger.''

Daniel stepped forward. ''It's all right, Kat. Granger was taken into custody before he entered the bank.'' He walked off to where a group of men in suits gathered near the bank.

''How?'' Kat looked up at Elizabeth.

''Well, the bright boy figured out what we were doing when he came home to an empty house.'' She beamed at Kat. ''Right away, he contacted the sheriff and they managed to sneak up on me.''

''Are you okay?''

''Oh, yes. Of course, it's terribly understanding of Sheriff Wade not to press charges against me.''

Kat sat upright. ''What?''

''Well, it was his own fault, sneaking up on me in the dark. I gave him what for with my purse.''

Kat grimaced. ''Oh, you didn't. That thing weighs a ton.''

''So he found out.'' Elizabeth sighed. ''They forced the story out of me, which is a good thing. Granger was nabbed before he knocked on the door.''

''I was afraid he'd find Daniel. There was no way to warn him.'' Kat shivered, remembering her feeling of helplessness.

''Heavens, no. Daniel had him on the ground and cuffed without a sound. Very professional, just like on television. Buster even helped.''

''How? He's back at the house.''

Elizabeth smiled. ''Daniel brought him and Buster charged Granger and took a bite out of his bottom.''

Kat continued to scan the crowd for Daniel. She needed to see for herself that he was unharmed. ''What about Chad?''

''He was blubbering like a baby the last time I saw him, shooting his mouth off about the whole setup as they pulled away. He'd better hope he's in a separate cell from that Granger.''

Kat eased her feet onto the ground and stood. Still no sign of Daniel returning to the car.

"He's not here, dear. Finished his report to the sheriff and left a few minutes ago."

Kat's heart plummeted. It wasn't a surprise, but it hurt. Now that the case was solved for his company, she had expected him to leave. But he could at least say goodbye.

Elizabeth patted Kat's hand. "I'm going to stay at Wilma's tonight. You make sure to have a nice cup of tea and get right to bed. Best thing for you." She walked away, arm in arm with the waiting Wilma.

Completely abandoned.

Sheriff Wade approached. "You okay, Miss Bennett?"

"I will be." Kat tilted her chin determined to hide her heartache.

"Good, good. I'll need you to come to the station in the morning to fill out a report."

"Okay." Kat wrapped her jacket tighter about her. A thump against her side reminded her of the recorder. ''Oh, this will probably help. I was able to record Chad Filcher.''

The sheriff accepted it with a wide smile. ''Concrete evidence, that's what I like to see.''

Kat smiled weakly. His words reminded her of Daniel. She wanted to go home and lick her wounds in private. Even the knowledge that her aunt's money would now surface didn't seem to matter.

She promised to make her report the next day and drove toward home. The windows were dark, shadowed, and she didn't want to go into the empty, lonely house. It held too many memories of Daniel.

But Buster waited and he'd been left alone too long. That is if Daniel had returned him to the house. Kat approached the front porch. No Buster.

Elizabeth was right. She had it bad. Kat wondered how long it would take her shattered heart to recover if she didn't go after Daniel. Several lifetimes no doubt. Why hadn't she taken a chance and shared with him how she felt.

Kat heard rustling from the porch swing as she placed her foot on the boards. She jumped. "I'm warning you—"

"I don't need another lump, Kat."

It was Daniel, not an errant bad guy looking for revenge. "You...I...how..." Kat stammered.

Her eyes adjusted to the soft moonlight filtering through the leaves of the aspen. The man had made her cry. Kat yanked a hair from his arm.

"Ouch! For crying out loud," Daniel rubbed his arm, "What was that for?"

"For scaring the life out of me, for making me think you left without saying anything, for making me love you—" Kat stopped, horrified to have revealed her heart. But hadn't she just been wishing she'd told the man when she thought he'd gone?

"Why do you think I'm here right now?" He stood and stepped closer. Only inches separated them.

"We're...physically...compatible."

"Yes." Daniel answered and took another step.

Her brows drew together. What was he trying to say?

"I've touched you. But I need more." Daniel cupped her cheek. "You've made me believe in unconditional love."

Kat's breath stopped for a split second. Her eyes widened. Was it possible? She swallowed and opened her mouth to speak.

"No. Let me finish." Daniel stopped her words before they could start. "I thought love meant giving up who I am, sacrificing individuality." He brushed his thumb over her lower lip. "You showed me that wasn't true. My suitcase is inside.''

A smile pulled at the corners of her mouth. ''How did you get rid of Elizabeth and Buster?''

''Buster is spending the night with a couple of rambunctious kids down the street.'' He shook his head. ''All I had to offer Elizabeth was to name our second born after Teddy Roosevelt.''

''Oh.'' Stunned, Kat stared up at him.

Daniel pulled her into his arms. ''I have to warn you, I intend to keep you out here until you accept a life sentence with me.''

''What are you saying, Mr. West?'' she squeaked.

His fingers threaded in her hair. ''I want to wake up with you every morning, learn about those bug parts you call tea, and make love to you in every room of this house.''

Kat focused on Daniel's words. ''You aren't leaving?''

"Earth to Kat," he teased, "I love you, woman. You won't get rid of me that easily. Besides, Miss Elizabeth mentioned you'd be singing show tunes in town square this week."

"Oh, Daniel. I love you, but I never dreamed you'd stay. I planned on talking to a Realtor in the morning about selling the business." Tears welled in her eyes. "I was going to follow you to Denver and make you love me."

"Soon as Sheriff Wade receives my paperwork, you're looking at the new Deputy Sheriff of Sugar Gulch. My background as a private investigator and my police training made me a good candidate." Daniel leaned back. "But there will be no more helping me on cases, Miss Bennett. My heart can't take the lumps."

Kat pulled him closer for a deep, soul-binding kiss. She pulled back an inch and tilted her head. "What was that remark about Teddy Roosevelt?"

Daniel nuzzled her neck. "I don't want you mad, but I had to promise Elizabeth we'd name our first female child after her when she caught me pawing through your lingerie."

"And the second?"

"Seems she has this fascination with Roosevelt. If that's a problem, I'm sure she'll give on one of them." His voice tapered off when his mouth lowered to her neck.

Kat pressed closer for a moment before taking his hand and leading him inside.

What had they been talking about? It didn't matter—Kat and Daniel had a lifetime to work out the details.

MILLS & BOON® PUBLISH EIGHT LARGE PRINT TITLES A MONTH. THESE ARE THE EIGHT TITLES FOR JUNE 2004

❦

SOLD TO THE SHEIKH
Miranda Lee

HIS INHERITED BRIDE
Jacqueline Baird

THE BEDROOM BARTER
Sara Craven

THE SICILIAN SURRENDER
Sandra Marton

PART-TIME FIANCÉ
Leigh Michaels

BRIDE OF CONVENIENCE
Susan Fox

HER BOSS'S BABY PLAN
Jessica Hart

ASSIGNMENT: MARRIAGE
Jodi Dawson

MILLS & BOON®

Live the emotion

0504 Rom LP

MILLS & BOON® PUBLISH EIGHT LARGE PRINT TITLES A MONTH. THESE ARE THE EIGHT TITLES FOR JULY 2004

———————— ❦ ————————

THE BANKER'S CONVENIENT WIFE
Lynne Graham

THE RODRIGUES PREGNANCY
Anne Mather

THE DESERT PRINCE'S MISTRESS
Sharon Kendrick

THE UNWILLING MISTRESS
Carole Mortimer

HER BOSS'S MARRIAGE AGENDA
Jessica Steele

RAFAEL'S CONVENIENT PROPOSAL
Rebecca Winters

A FAMILY OF HIS OWN
Liz Fielding

THE TYCOON'S DATING DEAL
Nicola Marsh

MILLS & BOON®

Live the emotion

0604 Rom